FAMILIAR STRANGERS

FAMILIAR STRANGERS

HAWTHORN ACADEMY BOOK ONE

D.R. PERRY

DISRUPTIVE IMAGINATION

LMBPN Publishing
PMB 196, 2540 South Maryland Pkwy
Las Vegas, NV 89109

Version 1.00, June 2021
(Previously published as a part of the megabook *Hawthorn Academy: Year One*)
ebook ISBN: 978-1-64971-833-4
Print ISBN: 978-1-64971-834-1

CHAPTER ONE

"Beware the Ides of June." I lifted my hand and touched the back of it to my forehead, tilting my head back in a melodramatic pose. "They herald impending disaster!"

I wasn't trying to be a drama queen, only distract my friends from the boring news broadcast about the Federal Bureau of Extrahumans arresting that evil extramagus from Rhode Island. Not a good look for a television hanging from an arcade's ceiling.

"Aliyah, honestly. It's only your birthday." Noah rolled his eyes. "I'd tell you to grow up, but that's pointless." His familiar, Lotan, poked her snaky head out of my brother's collar, sticking her forked tongue out at me.

"Don't be a dick, Noah." Izzy shrugged. "Anyway, Aliyah's sixteen today, not six. And her magic's at least as strong as yours, so watch yourself."

"But I'm her big brother." Noah flashed us all one of his stage-perfect smiles. "It's my job to give her grief, after all. She can't exactly hold it against me."

I took my hand off my forehead, made a fist, then used the other hand to make a cranking motion as I raised just one finger in my brother's general direction. You can guess which one.

"Hey, Miss, please don't do that in here."

I dropped my hands, turning to face the speaker. It was a broad-shouldered, dusky-complected, blue-haired guy in a Salem Willows apron. Great. Just what I needed on my birthday—a seasonal employee on my case for flipping the bird. He seemed to be about my age on top of it all, with melty brown eyes, perfect ringlets, and a chiseled jawline.

"Sorry, yeah, I know." Salem Willows Arcade has always been an all-ages environment. "I'll watch my figurative mouth while I'm here."

" I'm sorry, it's kind of my job to be a jerk. My manager really doesn't like it when parental units ask to speak to him." He shrugged. "Them's the breaks, I guess."

"Oh, good gracious me, is it really so awful working here?" Cadence folded her pale hands, then used them as a pedestal to rest one side of her head on. She blinked, her turquoise eyes like the sea. Which makes sense, 'cause she's a mermaid.

"Yeah, this is the best and worst summer job in Salem. But what can you do?" He shook his head. "This job is sort of a requirement for me."

"I guess everyone wants more money." Cadence sighed, sounding sympathetic. Practically everything she says, whether word or noise, comes off sounding like exactly what you want to hear. It's all part of her mermaid mojo. "Easy come, easy go."

"She wouldn't know anything about that." Noah turned his head, pausing beside the Skee-Ball machine. "Cadence's family is super-important. Rumor has it, they've got mountains of clams."

"Noah!" I tossed my crumpled straw wrapper at his head, and for once, he didn't manage to duck in time. "It's my freaking birthday, and you weren't invited, so just leave already."

"Whatever." Noah rolled his eyes for the five hundredth time that day. "You'll have to put up with me and my attitude at home later." He faked a pout. "So there."

And with that, my obnoxious older brother flipped his jet-black shoulder-length hair to one side, slapped his last token on my table, and sashayed toward the exit.

"What's his problem?" Izzy scooped up the token, bouncing it in her hand.

"I don't know. But you'd think he was my younger brother, the way he tags along everywhere we go." I chuckled. "And that attitude."

"He's your brother?" The curly-haired guy blinked. "That guy there?"

"Yup."

"I'm sorry."

"Oh, it gets worse." Cadence sighed, batting her eyes.

Why was she flirting with this guy? It shouldn't have mattered to me. She was the flirt of the group. I'm awkward and gangly, and Izzy just isn't interested in boys. Or girls either, for that matter.

"Do you know they're going to the same prep school in the fall?" Cadence dropped this line while somehow managing to brush right past the heartrending elephant in the room.

Which was that we three besties would suffer social amputation from each other, come September. But I couldn't blame her. I'd have tried forgetting that too if I could. That was impossible because Izzy, Cadence, and I had an epic friendship history that had started in kindergarten. We thought it would never die, but Izzy didn't talk about it all last year. For a divination psychic like her, that silence was a literal bad omen.

The Arcade's newest summer employee stood there with his mouth open like Cadence had slapped him in the face with a fistful of minnows instead of dropping hints about our educational apocalypse. He stared at me with eyes like fancy cups of coffee on saucers.

"First you tell me you're Noah Morgenstern's sister, then I find out you're starting Hawthorn Academy right along with me this fall?" He grinned. It looked so good on him, I wondered whether he was using a glamour or something. But he couldn't be. Changelings didn't go to Hawthorn. "Hi, I'm Dylan Kahn."

"And that's important because?" Izzy snorted. I noticed her hand inside the little black backpack she always carried. She was probably about to consult her cards. My psychic friend Isabella Mendez always brought sass along with her predictions.

"Because I don't know anyone here in Salem." He leaned against the table, speaking to me instead of my friends. "It's one reason I had to get a job this summer. My parents won't let me be a total introvert anymore."

"That's the lamest pickup line she's ever heard." Izzy slapped the card in her hand on the table face up. Thank goodness she didn't mention how it was almost the first pickup line I'd heard.

"Or maybe it's not a total failure." My psychic friend parted her fingers to show us the Two of Cups. It wasn't even reversed.

"Oh, Izzy." Cadence clucked like a mother seahen. "I don't think your card has anything to do with this fellow."

Dylan's jaw eased, like the words were a refreshing sea breeze. But then, my merfriend continued.

"Even if he is trying to flirt with our birthday girl," Cadence said, winking, "I've got mermaid's intuition that something else is going on here."

"Uh." Dylan's hands wrung the hem of his Salem Willows apron.

"Why?" Izzy tilted her head, eyes on the mermaid.

"Because that's the same card Noah got when he found Lo—" Cadence emitted a squeak like a dolphin's.

"Holy—"

"Mother—"

They were all cut off as I bolted out of my seat. Something touched my shoulder, and not just any something. It felt cold and slightly sticky, like a spiderweb, but it wasn't one. It was too thick and had sinew in it; strength, direction, and purpose. I sucked in air, just knowing I'd let it out in a scream the next instant.

If Salem Willows management would chew me out over flipping the bird, they might ban me all summer if I cussed a blue streak in there, so I did the only thing I could think of.

I bolted.

The Salem Willows Arcade had wide-open doors, like an auto garage except there were Skee-Ball and claw machines and video games inside. That made it easy to flee the scene plus what- or whoever had me by the shoulder. I didn't even have to dodge too

4

many people because elementary and middle schools were in session for another week.

Anyway, all this was beside the point because my attempted escape wasn't working.

The wind rushed past my ears, but behind me, something whooshed overhead. It was like getting dive-bombed by a seagull looking for errant tater tots, and the thing was still on my neck. I ran faster.

My feet just barely hit the pavement as I hightailed it out of there. I wasn't using magic. I conjure fire, not air. It was just a side effect of trying so hard to get away. The moment I reached the edge of the grass near the veterans' monument, I stopped, dropped, and counted on my friends to help me with whatever creepazoid had me by the shoulder. And also, the hair.

Except they didn't. Instead, I heard a trill from Cadence and wheezing snorts from Izzy. They laughed, which meant I wasn't in mortal danger, so of course, I lifted my heavier-than-usual head to see what was so funny.

And that was when I realized something was sitting on my head. Maybe more like perching. I almost batted it away when a red-gold scaled head, upside down, dangled in my face.

"Peep?"

"Sorry, I don't speak dragonet." I waved my hand. "Shoo!"

Yeah, that's right. A dragonet had goosed and chased me. And after all that, the little magical critter wouldn't leave me alone. The tiny winged lizard didn't shoo, scram, skedaddle, or get off my head. Just hung there, peeping in my face.

At least the critter held on with its claws retracted.

I waved both hands over my head this time. I didn't want to hit the dragonet but wanted its grip on my hair to release. The pulling sensation hurt a bit. I was rewarded for my effort by the critter plopping into my lap, strands of my obnoxiously brassy blonde hair dangling from the creature's toe scales. Both my pride and my intentionally messy bun were a wreck.

My friends had stopped laughing, at least. That was a good thing because I'd have told them to shut their traps. The dragonet sat up in my lap, tail flailing as one wing extended and the other dragged like a flag in a rainstorm. My stomach sank as I wondered whether this innocent creature had been injured because I'd freaked out.

"Poor thing, your wing's hurt." I reached out, offering it my arm because everybody knows you don't just grab animals or put your hands near their mouths. "Come on, I know just where to bring you."

The dragonet hopped up on my arm, favoring the injured wing. Rounding in the hindquarters suggested she was female and young—like me. I blinked my stinging eyes, hoping I could stop crying. I wasn't one of those super-expressive people, and I almost never tear up while reading or watching a movie.

Somehow, I practically felt the magical critter's pain and misery. No, that wouldn't do. Ember was her name. A wave of relief washed over me as I examined her injured wing, which was twisted, not broken, with a small red sore. Ember would recover if she got proper care.

"Where are you going, Lee?"

"To see Bubbe."

My friends followed as I headed toward my grandmother's office. None of us drive, and Salem Willows was a ways from downtown, but the dragonet's injury wasn't immediately life-threatening. Getting there in time would be a piece of cake.

We crossed Fort Avenue a block early to avoid Irzyk Park, also known as Tank Park because its main feature was a decommissioned military vehicle. The local shifter gangbangers hung out there, and Noah always told us to stay away. Cadence's parents agreed.

Cadence looked over her shoulder at the thankfully vacant area, something she'd never bothered with until just a couple of weeks ago. I hoped she wasn't thinking of introducing herself to the Tanks. That was what they called themselves. At least there was no such thing as a shark shifter, but you wouldn't have guessed that if you saw the way my aquatic friend stared.

"Cadence, quit it." Izzy, direct as ever, called the mermaid on the carpet.

"Just making sure the, um, unsavories aren't watching." She pointed out a crow perched on top of the tank. "Which maybe they are."

"Sure, whatever you say." Izzy snorted. She did that an awful lot, but I hardly blamed her. If she were a beverage, Izzy would be water. Direct, to the point, and exactly what you needed most of the time. Cadence was more like a cosmic coolatta.

Ember peeped again, clinging to my arm with little talons that were sharp like a baby's nails. I understood her renewed distress as we approached a busier area. Magical critters could camouflage themselves, but dragonets needed to fold their wings in order to look like mundane lizards. She couldn't, and that put her on edge.

Everybody had known about magic since before I was born anyway, so I wasn't worried about getting in trouble. Just about Ember getting nervous and hurting herself.

The only way I could help was by adjusting the strap on my bag so it hung partly in front of Ember's back and hindquarters. This settled her a bit, which was good because the last thing I wanted to do was drop her.

"Just a few more blocks, okay?" One corner of my mouth twitched, but I couldn't quite manage the reassuring smile Bubbe would have worn.

Ember blinked, then lowered her head to rest it on my arm. I took that as a good sign.

At the corner of Forrester and Hawthorne Street, we stopped for traffic and then crossed. Half a block down, we took a right after Izzy's house and headed behind it to number ten and a half. Bubbe's office was on the first floor, and my family all lived upstairs in the top two stories.

My arms were full, so Cadence opened the door for me. That was nice, even if she added in her signature flourishing curtsy to show off as I passed her. There was only one reason she'd showboat like this— someone was watching us. I looked over my shoulder.

All I saw was another crow perching on the awning of the antique shop across the street. Or maybe the same one; I know magical critters, not mundane birds. If it were a bad omen, Izzy would have said something. There was no time to ask Cadence about her sudden-onset aviary obsession with an injured dragonet in my arms.

CHAPTER TWO

Bubbe was in the back when we got inside. I knew because I heard her singing to one of her patients behind the door separating the exam room from the waiting area. That was no problem because she'd see we came in on the magipsychic security system. My grandma was pretty high tech for an older lady who'd learned her magic decades before the Great Reveal.

I sat down to wait, Ember cradled in my arms, and a less on-key rendition of the same tune Bubbe sang in the other room coming out of my mouth. It was a good thing I didn't want a performance art career. Some extrahuman folk have had great success along those lines, but I'd never be one of them, and that's okay.

I didn't want to be Irina Kazynski or Lane Meyer. Instead, I wanted Bubbe's job, which was helping animals. I just had to get a B+ average or higher at Hawthorn Academy so I could get into Providence Paranormal after I graduated.

Ember got downright clingy, tail curled around my arm like a copper bracelet as she leaned against me. She used my breastbone as a pillow, and it was absolutely adorable.

"You've got a new scaly bestie." Izzy peered at me from behind one of her tarot cards. I had no idea which one because it faced her. She put it away. "Familiar material."

"Yes, Isabella, you soothsaid all of this at the Arcade if I'm not mistaken." Cadence nodded in a way I assumed she believed was wise. Her chestnut curls bounced, making her look about as sage as a sorority pledge. Maybe that was a bad analogy, and not just because my Mer-friend looked nothing like Barbie. The gal from that movie about the blonde law student was in a sorority, and she had a giant brain, right?

"Maybe." Izzy shrugged. "That two of cups might have meant something else, but this is a sure thing. You and the scaly critter might already have a bond."

"That is so cool!" Cadence bounced on her toes. She did the same thing with her tail when she was in the ocean.

But my seagoing friend was only this expressive with positive emotions. All her turmoil (which I suspected was vast) stayed hidden. For about the millionth time, I wondered how she handled life with a foot on land and a fin under the sea. I probably wouldn't manage going between an exclusively magical school and my regular townie life as handily.

I was very thankful for my friends. We always got through everything together, before. For a hot minute, I dared to think this year would be no different.

And then all my gratitude toward the universe and its ineffable movements crashed around me as I remembered how I'd barely have time to see them once this summer was over.

Before I got maudlin enough for Izzy and Cadence to notice, Bubbe stepped through the door behind the counter.

My paternal grandmother wasn't all arms and legs like my mom and me. Instead, she was built along the same lines as Dad, which meant petite yet comfortingly solid. Her hair was bobbed and curly, a trait she also shared with my old man, but unlike him, she dyed all her gray in a variety of punk-rock hues. That week it was bubblegum pink.

Bubbe was my role model in just about everything, though biology had dictated long ago that I'd be nothing like her physically when I'm fully grown. At that moment, I couldn't imagine stronger life goals than following her career path.

She carried a dropper bottle filled with pearly blue liquid, which meant the critter in the back was another magical reptile. Bubbe's always had a soft spot for the critters most people avoid, like serpents, salamanders, spiders, and of course, dragonets.

"Bissel, who have you brought in today?" She peered down at the dragonet in my arms. I couldn't bring myself to roll my eyes at the diminutive, which meant "little bit."

"Bubbe, I'm practically a giant nowadays." The weak protest was all I could muster. I leaned forward, giving my grandmother a better view of my little friend. "Anyway, she's a dragonet. I'm calling her Ember for now."

"It's the wing, I see." Bubbe turned sideways, gesturing toward the door she'd emerged from. "Come along, girls."

I walked carefully past my grandmother and toward the door. Izzy and Cadence glanced at each other, hesitating. They'd never been invited into the back at Bubbe's. When Cadence took a step forward, Izzy put out a hand to stop her, but my grandmother shook her head.

"Isabella, you're like family here. Cadence, too. It's about time you got a look at how all of this works."

"Wow, thanks, Doc Morgenstern!" Cadence clapped her hands. I would have too if mine hadn't been full of small, cute, and scaly. I'd always wanted them to see how awesome extraveterinary medicine is.

"Yeah, thanks." Izzy's bluntness came from being brought up in a psychic shop, watching her parents work while being seen but not heard Of the three of us, she always fought change the hardest.

In the back, there was a hallway with a series of half-doors. What I mean is the doors all had bottoms and tops which open and closed separately. Most were closed all the way, but a few had only the bottoms shut. Bubbe called them Dutch doors.

I turned my head to the right as we passed the first half-open door.

Inside was a Grim. Those weren't the sort of magical animals who can be familiars. Instead, they're pure faerie creatures who usually live in the Under unless they've got an agreement with a psychic Summoner. Some of them were totally sentient like Gnomes or even smarter than average humans and extrahumans like Brownies, but Grims were pretty much like regular dogs. Plenty of folks were scared of them, but I always thought they were awesome.

"Whose is that, Bubbe?" I jerked my chin at the shadow beastie.

"Oh, I'm just sheltering this Grim here today as a favor to a visiting friend." Bubbe reached out and pulled the top half of the door closed. "Just for a rest while my friend is sightseeing. Too bright a day for an Unseelie creature to be out and about comfortably."

"That's awful nice of you, Doc Morgenstern." Izzy smiled, then elbowed Cadence. "So, I guess having psychic friends runs in your family."

Cadence gave Izzy a stiff sort of nod.

"And merfolk, too, Cadence." I reached out to grab her hand, squeezing. Her smile widened as it eased. "Anyway, it's really nice of you to help like that, especially during the summer when it's busy, Bubbe."

"It's not quite so hectic yet." My grandmother dropped us all a wink.

As if to disprove her point, a tinkle of chimes sounded in the air beside Bubbe's head. She tapped one of the moonstone studs in her earlobe and the music stopped.

"Magipsychic earrings! Cool!" Cadence beamed again.

The merfolk had spent most of the last thirty years avoiding us landlubber extrahumans and all the integration we've done with the rest of the world's population. Her family was one of only a few who had living space on land. She said it was because her family did important diplomatic work with the land-dwellers.

My grandmother blinked three times, activating the device that let her see the waiting room. I was shaky on the details of how that worked because I was a future animal doctor, not a magipsychic engineer. Whatever she saw out there had her turning on her heel and power-walking back up the hall. Of course, I followed her all the way out into the waiting room.

Big mistake.

Standing at the counter was a gaggle of magi, all girls about my age. The two waiflike brunettes were identical twins, while the redhead in the middle looked totally unrelated. They had on enough makeup for a red-carpet premiere.

All three of them wore actual designer clothes, and I realized they were in town on vacation. From New York City, judging by their accents, and uptown, based on their hairstyles and jewelry.

The non-twin carried an oversized Hermes tote, its top level with the surface the girl leaned on. I saw a platinum luggage tag bearing an engraved Park Avenue address.

A sleek snout with a curving canine muzzle poked out of it, followed by the head of an Egyptian Sha disguising itself as a small dog. Its ebony and gold familiar's collar gleamed against its short dark gray fur, more ornate than it had to be but unmistakable all the same. It sniffed before I noticed its gaze fall squarely on Ember's busted wing.

The crested canine Sha tended to gravitate toward magi with undeath, umbral, or poison magic, which were all on the opposite spectrum from my own fire magic. So of course, the animals reacted to each other like oil and water.

As the Sha made a yappy racket, I sighed. Maybe my eyes rolled. The other girl started huffing and puffing and threatening to ask for the manager.

"How stupid can you be, bringing a dragonet around a Sha like that? That beast isn't even your familiar. Is this an extraveterinary office or an underground animal fight club? Honestly. I ought to take my business somewhere else."

"It'd be nice if you could, Miss Fairbanks. However, Hawthorn Academy's got its familiar licensing contract with my office. Here's the required form." Bubbe pushed a piece of paper across the counter toward the girl, shooting what I call "the look" at the Sha. It shut its mouth, of course. All critters did when Bubbe made that face.

"Whatever. Just have your moronic assistant get that scaly menace out of here." She turned her nose up. "Or I'll be back on our next long weekend up here with my father. And you're well aware of how connected he is."

Miss Park Avenue was threatening Bubbe.

Her words burned. And yeah, it started getting hot in there because that's what happens to fire magi like me when we're angry. I took a deep breath, about to tell this girl who she's talking to and why she should stop it.

Ember whimpered. When I looked down at her, she had the most miserable expression on her face, like Dad got when I let him down in some way.

And just like that, I banked all that shame and anger to the lowest levels I could manage. When I said "bank," I used the double meaning. One thing my mom taught me about fire magic is this: you can't just lock it up indefinitely. It's got to come out sooner or later, or that inferno will eat you alive.

But that day, with a hurt animal in my arms, was not the time.

I turned my back, striding with as much of my shaken confidence as I could muster toward the door Izzy held open. My upper lip was stiff, chin up, head held high.

It was all a show, but a good one, I hoped.

"That's what I thought." The alpha mean-girl scoffed.

"You showed her, Faith."

"True story." Faith laughed. I listened to the scratch of pen on paper as she filled out the forms for her Sha. At least she seemed to care about her familiar.

As Izzy stepped aside, letting go of the door, Faith Fairbanks delivered her parting shot.

"I'll show her even more at school in September."

I didn't return fire. It would have been literal, and I didn't want to burn down Bubbe's lobby. I had no idea why this girl had taken a few barks and hisses so personally, but as I headed into an exam room with Ember in my arms and my best friends at my side, I knew one thing.

I'd have to handle anything Faith Fairbanks decided to dish out on my own. Noah wouldn't get in the middle of a dispute between first-years.

Happy birthday to me.

CHAPTER THREE

In July, we were in the middle of the hottest week on record in Salem. Izzy, Cadence, and I had already seen all three movies at Cinema-Salem. None of our parents could drive us to the Danvers Mall, and anyway, they didn't allow dragonets in there.

There was one place left for us to go have fun: Salem Willows, of course. We were there half the week but didn't mind making another trip. It had Izzy's favorite game and people-watching for Cadence—and a future fellow Hawthorn attendee I really ought to try harder to befriend.

"So, you're back for more Skee-Ball, I see." Dylan Kahn waved as he approached. "You three are practically fixtures in here."

"It's an arcade, and we're still kids." Izzy chuckled, brandishing a ten-dollar bill. "Now, give me all your tokens!"

"Technically kids, you mean." Cadence examined her nails like she didn't want to be here. But I caught her stealing glances at the chrome-sided machines with their particolored flashing lights.

"Whatever." I shrugged. Ember gripped my shoulder tighter, struggling to keep her balance. "Oops, sorry about that, girl."

"Peep."

"What's that mean?" Izzy planted her feet in front of her Skee-Ball lane, preparing to roll.

"I think she said something like okay." I headed to the next row, where I helped the dragonet perch above the ball return so she could watch.

"So why isn't she your familiar yet, Aliyah?" Dylan leaned against a support beam. The Willows had plenty of those, and he made good use of them.

"I'm not sure?" I shook my head. "I think my parents expected me to bond with a Tallin like Dad and Noah."

The little split-tailed sun serpents dated at least as far back as the Old Testament days. The Morgensterns have been associated with them for just as long.

"Well, what about Bubbe?" Cadence grinned. "Doesn't she have one of those little snakies too?"

"She did until last fall, and her next one's probably going to be the same type." I put the token into the slot and listened to the balls roll down.

"So, either Ember's the anomaly, or you are." Izzy's bluntness hit me like a lead pipe to the head. She sank her first ball into the five-hundred-point slot, too. Skee-Ball was totally her game. Always has been.

"None of the above." I took a shot and managed one hundred points. "It could just be a dragonet thing. Maybe they imprint or something. Bubbe said she must have hatched the day we tangled, or maybe the one before."

"Wow." Cadence twisted one of her shell bracelets. "Ember's practically a baby, then."

"I can't believe your grandma lets you bring her everywhere." Dylan rummaged in his apron, collecting the tokens Izzy already paid for. "Lucky."

"The fresh air is good for her." I rolled my second ball, which landed in the gutter.

"How come we haven't seen your familiar, Dylan?" Izzy sank a ball for one hundred points.

"Uh, well." He cleared his throat. "You all get to come here for fun. I'm working."

"I see." Izzy snorted before glancing up at our scores. "Come on, Aliyah. Keep rolling."

I did, but no matter what, I couldn't catch up to Izzy that day. Cadence did better, but our psychic friend managed to squeak out a victory by a scant five points.

"Well, I'm out of tokens and money."

"And I'm practically drying up in this heat." Cadence fanned herself with a flier from the Engine House, where we usually went after a day at the arcade. But the mermaid had other ideas. "Let's go swimming. Dylan, too."

"Dylan what now?" He'd just come back from handing his apron to the manager.

"Come out with us." Cadence smiled.

"Yeah." I nodded. "You've been in town for over a month now, and I've never once seen you do anything just for fun."

"Well, that's because I've got to save my money and stuff."

"Swimming is free." I flashed him a grin. "Perfect for the teenager on a budget."

"Peep!" Apparently, Ember was happy with the choice of activity. Even fire dragonets enjoyed swimming, which made sense because in the wild, they'd catch and eat fish to survive.

"Come on, Ember." I held my arm out so she could make her way up to my shoulder. "And come on, Dylan."

"I don't have a swimsuit."

"I have brothers." Izzy tucked the tickets she'd won into the back pocket of her cutoffs. "They're younger, but Matteo's the same size as you."

"Okay, then."

We headed back toward downtown Salem and Hawthorne Street. Cadence led the way, a spring in her step as we passed Irzyk Park. Once again, I didn't see anyone hanging around, but the big black bird was back, cawing and flapping its wings.

"What's with that raven?" Dylan jerked his thumb at the feathered fiend.

Izzy scoffed. "Probably found something tasty in the garbage."

"Hey, don't assume." I shook my head. "Ravens can be familiars sometimes, especially for air magi." I glanced at Dylan.

"Yeah, no. Not me." His cheeks reddened. "I mean, I'm air but no ravens. After reading that Poe poem, they sort of freak me out."

"Huh." Cadence's voice had a lilt to it I'd only ever heard when she discussed boys. "I think they're cool. Mysterious, you know?" She fluttered her fingers at the bird, which stopped its hopping and stared.

"Well, clearly that one's intelligent." I made a mental note to remind Bubbe to check for nests. "Anyway, it's too hot to stand around here bird-watching."

"Yeah, I guess." Cadence flipped her ponytail to the other side of her neck. "Let's get the clothes and go swim already."

She hurried off, ending up on the porch at Izzy's house. The mermaid sulked on the porch while the psychic fetched Matteo's extra swim trunks for Dylan. After that, she headed back inside to change.

I beckoned to Cadence and Dylan, leading them up the driveway between numbers ten and eleven. I gestured at the stoop, and they sat. When he saw the number placard beside the door, Dylan chuckled.

"Wow. I didn't know half addresses existed stateside. Mom would lose her mind if she knew."

"Why not show her, then?" Cadence pointed back down the driveway. "Even my folks have come to see this, and they hate walking when they don't have to."

"Well, they're back in London, working." He stared at Bubbe's van, the fence behind it, and then his shoes. "I'm here by myself."

"Oh, I had no idea." I fumbled with the keys, all butterfingers as I tried to open the door I've used on my own for most of my life. "Where are you staying?"

"Down at the Y. The one for magi."

"Ugh, I heard their cafeteria sucks." I shook my head. "I'll bring down some snacks for all of us. Swimming is hunger-making."

Finally, I pulled the door open and headed up the stairs two at a time. Being too tall has some advantages. Ember clung to my shoulder, her tail wrapped under my armpit.

Once inside the apartment, I jogged through the kitchen and then up the back stairs to the top floor. Once Ember was perched safely on my headboard, I rushed through changing, whipping my clothes off and whisking them into the hamper.

Rummaging through my drawers, I found my trusty swimsuit, a royal blue one-piece with racerback straps and a built-in sports bra.

And I found it too short to pull the straps past my bust.

"Oh, come on!" I growled, frustrated by the fabric. "You fit last month! Ugh. It's not you, it's me."

"You okay, Aliyah?"

I turned, arms crossed over my chest.

"It doesn't fit, Mom. And everyone's going swimming." I sniffled. "Stupid teenage hormones being all—stupid."

"We'll fix this." She beckoned. "Come along."

"Huh." I snagged a tissue from the box on my dresser and followed her, dabbing my cheeks and wiping my nose. "With magic?"

"Not exactly." Mom pushed the door of the room she shared with Dad open. "With a belated birthday present."

She headed toward the cedar wardrobe that's sat in the corner for as long as I can remember. I avoided the thing whenever possible because one of my earliest memories is of Noah shutting himself in there by accident, trying to get into the Under and meet a Sprite.

And there I was, standing in front if its intricately carved and matte-finished surface, face all red and sticky from crying. The earlier incident had been a way better reason to cry because as hard as I tugged, I couldn't get the door open to let my brother out of there. And he kept saying he couldn't breathe.

This July day's upset was over a perfectly normal bathing suit I'd grown out of seemingly overnight.

Mom finished rummaging and turned around, handing me a bag from Queen of Hearts in Providence, Rhode Island. That was where my mother came from, even though she never talked about it. I knew more about my great-grandpa escaping Nazis than about Mom's childhood in the Ocean State. So, how'd she get something from there in a bag and not an online order box?

Since Mom worked from home almost all the time and I had been at Salem Middle School every day last year, she could have taken a trip pretty easily. It was two and a half hours on the commuter rail and less than two in a car from Salem to Providence. The jaunt was even shorter via magical conveyance.

I stood there staring at the bag and forgetting just about every-thing in an attempt to remember one shred of info about Mom. Had she mentioned going out of town without us over the spring?

"Would you like to open it?" She had one hand out, palm up and pointing at the bag. The other was in a white-knuckled fist by her side.

I heard her voice, but the words didn't register. It was the same as trying to hear Noah through the wardrobe door all those years ago.

"Peep?" The sound came with a red-gold tail waving near my arm, tapping the back of my hand like the dragonet was asking if I was okay when she was the one with the twisted wing.

"I'm okay." I looked down at Ember and back up at Mom. "And yeah. I'll open it. I just never heard of this store before," I lied. Everyone knew where it was. "Is it a new place? Maybe in Portsmouth or Boston?"

"Providence." Her lips turned up, but Mom's eyes weren't smiling. She wasn't happy that I'd caught her out, then. I dropped that subject.

I reached into the bag, pushing past gilt tissue paper. In seconds, my fingertips brushed smooth and stretchy fabric. I gripped and pulled, revealing a turquoise and royal blue tankini. The bottoms were horizontal striped boy-shorts, and the top was printed with a Celtic knotwork pattern featuring dragons.

I ran one finger along the outline of a wing, noticing how much it resembled Ember when she stretched.

"Mom, this is—I mean, thanks so much." My throat tightened, choked up by a silly bathing suit. At that point, I didn't care anymore whether Mom had gotten it on some day trip she'd never told me about. "It's perfect."

"Run along and change now." This time when she smiled, Mom's whole face lit up.

I dashed into my room and changed into the new suit. Ember followed, peeping cheerfully. It fit perfectly, and because it was two pieces, getting taller wouldn't be a problem. I threw a maxi dress over it and slipped sandals on, then I held my arm down for Ember to climb up. After a quick check in the mirror, I grabbed my beach bag and hustled out of my room.

"Love you, Mom!" I hollered down the hall.

"To the Under and back," she replied.

For the rest of the day, I only went to the beach. Dylan headed into the park's bathroom to change out of his work clothes. Izzy braided her thick acorn-brown hair into two buns, one behind each ear, as usual. Cadence gazed at the sky, so I pointed out clouds with interesting shapes, but she wasn't in the mood for chatter. Ember butted her head against my cheek, begging for chin scratches.

We spent some of our time wading down by the park. Izzy wore the same old triathlon suit, and Dylan kept on his muscle shirt with his borrowed trunks. I tucked my maxi dress into the beach bag, sauntering along without a care because my new suit was so comfortable.

Cadence, of course, didn't need to change clothes. The seawater turned her legs scaly wherever it hit them, something that didn't happen with rain or tap water. When we finally went in, she let her legs fully shift into a tail and then swam rings around the three of us.

Cadence always seemed so free in the ocean; water's literally her element. She never went out far enough to really get going. It was because her parents wouldn't allow that until she was older.

It was nice to get into the water and cool off, but the northern Atlantic temperatures meant most of us couldn't stay in for long. Dylan managed for longer than I'd expected. When he emerged, he shivered so hard I gave him my towel.

We sat in a line on the tide wall, legs dangling and bags between us like beads on a string. I was still puzzled by Dylan's ability to tolerate the chilly water, so I asked him.

"I'm an air magus." He shrugged. "My parents taught me that if I wanted to be any good with this element, I'd need to try tolerating both heat and cold."

"Well, if you need practice with the heat part, Aliyah's an expert." Cadence grinned.

"I bet she's getting rusty with magic." Izzy side-eyed Cadence like an onion ring that fell on the floor. "All that time babysitting scaly critters, you know."

"Am not." I snorted. "Not that I can give you a demonstration or anything."

"I wouldn't think of asking." Dylan nodded. "Not in the middle of summer."

Cadence watched me like a seagull over a picnic table. Izzy sighed and tapped one finger on the concrete under her hand, eyes wide and mouth small, like she gets while trying to solve a math problem. I wasn't sure what all the fuss was about. Dylan seemed as clueless as I was.

Magical creatures were so much easier.

"Peep?" Ember poked her head out of my beach bag, one of my hair ties sitting on top of her head like some kind of pretty floral bonnet.

Everybody laughed, even,Ember, in a chirpy dragonet sort of way.

And just like that, the silence went from awkward to friendly. It stayed that way between the four of us all summer.

CHAPTER FOUR

A week into August, I paced my bedroom. That wasn't as easy as it had been last summer. I had always been gangly, limbs longer than they ought to be, but this year, I'd gotten extra tall on top of it. I bumped into people and things more than at any previous time in my life.

My ceiling was gabled, with slanting at the corners so the roof drained and let go of snow properly in the New England climate. As a little kid, I'd loved this. I'd made tents by tacking old sheets to the edges I could reach. But for pacing as a string-bean teen, it felt like courting a concussion.

I was about to give up when someone knocked on my door. Four quick taps, which meant Dad. Leaning slightly while reaching let me open it from where I stood.

"What's up, Aliyah?" He bent his knees a little as he craned his neck. My father didn't smirk about his dad joke, just showed a slight smile.

"Stuff. Things." I shrugged, feeling like a giraffe in a railway car. "Whatever."

"Why don't you come on downstairs and visit Bubbe with me?" He leaned on the doorframe, turning that smile up a notch.

I took a step before remembering my grandma had asked me to

run some errands for her yesterday. That always meant she wanted me out of her hair at the office. "Um, I thought she had a full house down there?"

"Mom and I talked to her last night, and that's not exactly the case."

"Well, what's the deal, then?"

"She's got a tricky surgery this morning."

"All the more reason to stay out of her way." I shook my head, not sure what my father was getting at. "What's your point?"

"You are. Look at you, worrying."

"I'm sixteen and going to a new school. Without my best friends. Of course, I'm worried."

"Are you sure that's what's got its hooks in you today?"

"Uh." I blinked. "No. Actually, I've got no idea what my problem is right now."

"Your mother's got a theory about a certain dragonet."

Mom's theories were no joke. That had been her college major, after all—theoretical magic.

"Ember? She's just an injured stray I brought to Bubbe. I've been doing that for years, Dad. No big deal."

"That may well be, but this surgery I mentioned is to fix her wing."

"Oh." I sat down on the edge of my bed.

"Your mother thinks coincidence had a hand in your finding her on your sixteenth birthday. We all think Ember's your familiar, Aliyah. It's time to test that, and if it's true, make things official."

As if to drive home his point, I got a twinge near my left shoulder. That might not sound strange since aches and pains happened all over the bodies of growing people, but it wasn't a spot on my body hurting. It was like phantom pain, except in a limb anyone who's not a flying shifter doesn't have. It was near my left shoulder, sure—off to the side, exactly where the first knuckle joint on a dragonet's wing would be.

"Ow?"

"I hate to say I told you so." My father shrugged. "But, well..."

"No, you don't, Dad." I smirked to show him there are no hard feelings. I didn't think my father hated anything.

"What else is new?" Dad turned his back, but not before I caught him smiling.

"Point."

I left my room and followed him down the hall toward the stairs that led down from the third floor with its four bedrooms and full bathroom. I didn't mind that Dad knew more than me. With Mom, it was a different story.

Mom was gentle and kind but always seemed sad somehow. And back then, nobody told me why. The handful of times I asked Dad or Bubbe outright, they said she'd tell me herself when she was ready.

I breathed a sigh of relief as we avoided her, continuing down the back stairs of the building instead of stopping on the second floor, which has our kitchen, dining, and living spaces, and Mom's office space. I heard her in there, talking to the principals at Salem High, Gallows Hill Hall, and Wolf Messing Prep on a clairvoyant device. One of her jobs was previewing the magical curricula for the schools around here.

Salem High wasn't specifically for extrahumans, but they were required by law to provide special courses for any students who weren't strictly human. Mostly, magical kids going there couldn't afford the prep schools and didn't have the grades for a scholarship. They spent a fifth year there, just for them, learning enough about their powers to do magical majors at college.

Izzy was going to Wolf Messing Prep down the road in Peabody. It was a day school for young psychic folks. They had some of the best courses in the United States for mentalists like clairvoyants and telepaths. Psychics whose powers were physically based, like telekinetics, had to go all the way to Copperfield College Preparatory in Las Vegas if they wanted a specialized education.

Gallows Hill was the local school for shifters. They'd let Cadence in because technically she shapeshifts. She said it had to be better to be the only mermaid at a school full of folks who switched between skin and fur or feathers than kids who just didn't get it.

Gallows Hill had recently opened their admissions to include any rare type of extrahuman but also Changelings since the Seelie and

Unseelie courts had reconciled. That whole business had happened thanks to the students and faculty at Providence Paranormal College. I wasn't entirely sure what they did or how they did it, but the group of them managed to take down a few seriously powerful bad guys in the process.

You'd think rational adults would consider them to be awesome role-models, but Dad was ambivalent, while Mom seemed uneasy whenever I gushed about how cool they all were. Even the very first mundane human to ever attend college there.

Mom loves that I've got such great friends in Cadence and Izzy, but she always asked why I never seemed drawn to other magi my age. I always told her it was because the ones in town were either younger or older than me. Hiding my anxiety about fitting in wasn't easy, but that summer, I realized Mom was almost as nervous as me about it. But she worked in the education field. She must have thought starting a magical prep school was the most important thing in the world.

Good thing Bubbe didn't tell her about my brand-new feud with Faith Fairchild. I hoped to smooth things over once school started. "That doesn't seem likely."

"What's that, Aliyah?" His hand hovered over the latch at the back entrance to Bubbe's office.

"My inside voice being an idiot again, Dad." I rolled my eyes. "Sorry. It wasn't directed at you." I stared at my feet, inexplicably frustrated. Was this what Noah meant when he cursed teenage hormones? Or was Dad right about me experiencing Ember's feelings?

"I understand that the eye roll is part of the teenage nonverbal landscape. No worries." His smile was like a calm sea. "But you said something doesn't seem likely, which reminds me of that old Magic 8 Ball you and Izzy used to play with. Is there something you want to talk about?"

"No." I shook my head.

"Okay." He opened the door and held it, standing aside for me.

I silenced the growl that was trying to escape my throat. At that point, I was convinced. He was right; this fear and anger had nothing to do with the situation I was in. It came from somewhere else. Some*one* else. Ember.

We strode down the hall at Bubbe's. Scuttling around on the floor inside one of the boarding rooms was a pastel-blue dragonet, rounded scales shimmering like cirrus clouds in an otherwise empty sky. His hindquarters were decidedly triangular, unlike Ember's. Also, he wore a gold and silver braided collar that designated him as someone's familiar.

"Whose critter is that, Dad?" I always asked questions in here, but that time I was extra curious. Dragonets were uncommon, so seeing another one was rare, even in a magical town like Salem.

"I'm not entirely sure." He shook his head. "But he's a friendly little guy. His magus must be missing him terribly."

"Hmm." The one thing that could distract me from an animal in trouble was a second one in need of aid. I almost suggested that we head over to Hawthorn Academy to ask around about a lost dragonet, but it was too late for that.

Somewhere behind the door leading into Bubbe's surgery, Ember shrieked.

I pushed past Dad and barged in, slamming the door open so hard it nearly hit me in the face on the backswing. I wasn't usually that aggressive, and the look on Bubbe's face had me wondering if maybe I went too far.

"Aliyah." Her jaw squared, hinting at the smooth, angular line it must have made when she was a much younger woman. "This isn't a pleasant event. Are you sure you want to be here for this?"

Ember let out a wail so desperate I could do nothing but rush to where she sat swaddled against the surgical steel table. Her injured wing was exposed, sticking out of an intentional hole in the muslin wrap holding her captive. I saw what was wrong with her. The sprain had healed, but the small lump near the joint turned into a bulging cyst. It had to be lanced, or Ember might never fly again.

I knew better than to try releasing her from the restraints or even touch her since everything had been sterilized, but I knew for sure that she needed me here. The whole situation was confusing for her, and she must have expected more pain. Anyone familiar with dragonets would recognize that pleading expression on her reptilian features. But it was not just how she looked that clued me in.

I could palpably feel just how much my presence in the room, where she could see me, helped Ember.

"I'm staying, Bubbe."

"As you wish, Bissel."

"But Mom!" I blinked a breath before Bubbe interrupted my father. He almost never called her that.

"No buts out of you, Aaron Uriel Morgenstern." Bubbe turned toward the sink, where she finished scrubbing up. "This is still my office and my surgery. Your daughter stays, and if you've got an issue with that, you go."

"No issue, Mom."

"And as for you, Aliyah, sit there, on the stool near the table. Put on a mask. Don't touch the patient until I say so."

"Okay, Bubbe."

I got a mask and followed her instructions. Dad leaned against the wall behind me. As we settled in and watched my grandmother, it became clear that this would be different from the last time I'd sat in on a surgery.

This wasn't my first animal hospital rodeo. When I was seven, Bubbe started taking my desire to be an animal doctor seriously. She'd also let me into the business side of her office for the first time back then, too. Over the last nine years, I'd seen pretty much everything.

Including a handful of patients she wasn't able to save.

Mom didn't much like that. She said it was nothing she'd have wanted to see when she was my age.

"You're not me, Aliyah. Go your own way," was what she told me back then. Mom believed in different strokes for different folks. It was the one filament of coolness twisted around the rest of her too-serious nature.

I let out the breath I'd been holding. Yes, I was aware of not breathing, thanks. And I'd hydrated earlier too because self-care is important. So is taking care of those who can't help themselves, which was the main reason I tried to help keep a dragonet from wigging out.

Looking Ember in the eye wasn't easy from where I sat, so I pulled the lever on the bottom of the stool to lower it. Once I reached eye level, I gazed at her scaly, angular face until she noticed I was there, which was practically immediately. She was a bright little thing.

"Peep." The sound was low and dull instead of that first bright chirp on the day I found her. Or maybe it was the other way around.

"I know, Ember." I gazed at the eye she turned toward me, wondering what was going on on the other side of that coppery iris with its vertical pupil. "We'll do something fun after this, okay? Maybe visit your buddy."

"That's right. Once you're better, you two can have a playdate." Dad grinned.

Bubbe called on her solar magic with a few words in Polish. The energy felt like the afternoon sun in winter. She imbued a scalpel with a crystal blade, one of the few instruments that would work on a very young magical creature like Ember without doing more harm than good. Even magi could never be sure exactly what kinds of magic they had, so using any metal on them was a risk, considering the various supernatural and elemental weaknesses they might suffer.

Metals, especially alloys like steel, were like rubbing peanut oil on every baby in a human maternity ward. You couldn't possibly know which one was allergic to what.

"Ember, I won't lie." I held out a hand, palm up. "This is going to hurt. But my grandma's the best doctor around."

"Peep." Ember nodded, and I felt her comprehension. Bubbe took hold of the injured wing with her free hand. The little dragonet shivered briefly, and I got the impression that for her, fear was cold.

"I'm making you a fire." I squinted at my outstretched hand, concentrating. "This is just for you. Watch the flames, and before you know it, this whole thing will be over, and you'll get better. Okay?"

She blinked as orange and yellow lit up the hollow of my palm. The center wasn't blue since I wasn't that powerful yet, but that didn't bother Ember.

As Bubbe's scalpel met Ember's cyst, they hissed in tandem. Through my flames, I saw a gout of greenish fluid erupt from the incision.

"Easy now, almost through." Bubbe's voice was low but flat as though she didn't like what she saw in the wound.

She set the scalpel aside and picked up a bottle of saline to rinse the incision. Once that was done, she applied an adhesive bandage treated with an herbal ointment mixed specially for dragonet scales. I exhaled. Ember joined in. The flames in my hand guttered.

"There." Bubbe tidied the table, tossing some items in the trash and others in a basin of rubbing alcohol.

"Can I hold her now?"

"Let's get the restraints off her first."

I put my fire out and helped. Green liquid from the cyst stained the fabric. It had an odor like stagnant ponds choked with algae. Bubbe took a few swabs and set aside samples for testing later. Maybe someday we'd get an idea of what had caused the injury.

Ember peeped a few times before settling her head in the hollow between my collarbone and trapezius muscle. I cradled her there, marveling at how even with the bandage, she could fold both wings fully against her back. In the right light, she'd be mistaken for a mundane lizard, but warm-blooded.

In moments she was snoring, tiny tendrils of smoke rising from her nostrils and making a foggy haze around my head.

"I think that about says everything." Dad nodded at Ember. He'd been so quiet I'd almost forgotten he was there.

"Yes." Bubbe sighed. "Yes, it does." She turned her back, busying herself with the simple task of cleaning. I couldn't blame her for playing the stoic now. Bubbe's familiar had passed on just last year, so of course, this was hard on her. Her knuckles whitened as she clutched the trash bag. "Well, go on then, Aaron." And she headed out of the room.

As my father stepped forward, holding the gold and silver braided collar, I watched his hands go through the formal motions as he murmured his binding incantation. Each magus used the language most significant to them. Dad's was Hebrew. A soft glow of solar magic that felt like midday in an apple orchard surrounded his hands.

Comforting sunlit energy enfolded me and the dragonet like a warm hug. A thread of fire magic flowed between us like we were the filament in an incandescent lightbulb.

As he fastened the collar around Ember's neck, I felt closer to the little dragonet than ever. A tear or three rolled down my face, blazing a trail through the ashes smudging it. I hadn't even noticed my fire magic leaving traces, but for once, I had an excellent excuse.

One glance at Dad told me there was something wrong, but not what.

He was crying.

Not a few drops of relief like my own tears. This was grief, like the night I barely remembered when we got the knock on the door. An officer in dress uniform stood in the hall and told us Dad's father had passed. But this was different somehow. Farther back than that grief.

I had no idea what was so painful about my bonding with a familiar at an appropriate age. His Tallin, Lyssa, grandmother of my brother's serpentine familiar, was with him that moment, peeking out of his shirt pocket.

"Dad?"

"Peep?" Ember queried in her sleep.

"I'll be okay." Dad sniffled, raising his sleeve to his face. Lyssa hissed, waving a handkerchief at him with her forked tail. "You just reminded me of something. Someone. A long time ago. Thanks." He took the square of fabric and made use of it.

He left a load of information out, but until he was ready to talk about it, there was nothing I could do. That went double for Bubbe, who I heard sniffling on the other side of the door.

CHAPTER FIVE

"Aliyah!"

Someone called my name in the dark, the cozy warm dark where my feet weren't remotely cold for once. A repeat performance of my name told me who was hollering it.

"Shut up, Noah. Mmmsleepin'." I tugged at the down-alternative filled comforter, pulling it farther over my head.

"How can you sleep at a time like this?" My jerkface brother yanked my blanket in the opposite direction. The bastard.

"Whahoozit?"

I had no choice but to sit up, blindly flailing around for my now-out-of-reach bedding. I winced as my wrist made contact with my bedpost. Bedpost? Crap. I committed a sin against gravity and overextended. Again.

"Oww!" My hip smacked against hardwood as I fell out of bed. Even barely awake, I was a klutz.

"Peep!" The whoosh of wings past my head made me chuckle. Yeah, Ember totally dive-bombed my big brother.

"You've meddled in the affairs of a dragonet, Noah!" I snorted.

"Dealing with dragons is totally different from dealing with dragonets. Anyway, I'm not crunchy, and ketchup's utterly basic." He ducked and covered. "Even your winged monstrosity knows it."

"Peep?" Ember perched on top of his head, blinking.

"Let him go, girl." I flashed her a grin. "He's done his worst here."

My room was already a disaster area. That was what happened when I procrastinated and left packing for dorm life until the last minute. Ember glided back to her favorite perch on my headboard.

"Is this really all you're bringing?" Noah aimed a withering glare at the rolling suitcase next to the door.

"Why? Do you think I'll need more than that?"

"This would fit under an economy seat, Aliyah."

Noah clicked his tongue, making a beeline for my closet. After opening the door, he stepped back, mouth wide with shock. Even his serpent Lotan pulled back into a near-strike position, forked tongue flickering.

"Everything's still here!" He pulled a dress-swaddled hanger off the rail inside. "There's no excuse for not bringing this."

Noah shook the mint-green dress almost cruelly before dropping it at the foot of my bed. A purple and orange broomstick skirt that he'd picked out for me in the hippie shop down at the Wharf joined it. More dresses, skirts, and a few blouses I almost never wore finished off the pile. He even tossed in a cardigan, the kind with little fabric-covered buttons.

"That's more than what I already packed."

"You'll be wanting all of this."

"It's only five days of classes. I'll be spending most of this one in pajamas anyway. I plan to go straight to my room after the welcome assembly."

"You absolutely will not. I'll be introducing you to some upper-classmen, and then you may go and change. Not into pajamas, either. You'll want something festive." He snagged my other suitcase—the one we brought on long weekends to Bar Harbor—off the floor of the closet. He began folding each item in half, hanger and all, before stowing them in there.

After a moment, he glanced at my bureau.

"Hey, no rummaging around in there." I shook my pointer finger at him. "I already packed socks and underwear, thank you very much."

"Well then, where in the world do you keep your accessories?"

I jerked my chin at the inside of the closet door, where the handful of necklaces I own hang on hooks.

"You don't have any scarves?" He feigned shock. "Blasphemous! I'll lend you a few of mine."

Noah trotted across the hall into his room and returned in under ten seconds. The variety of scarves in his arms told me he'd been planning this wardrobe intervention at least all morning, and possibly even all week.

"I can't believe you're not letting me choose my own clothes." I rolled my eyes. "We're allowed to wear whatever we want under our school blazers, after all."

"Oh, but I did, for the most part." He chuckled, waving at my much smaller bag. "All of this is just for special occasions."

"Look, you might like parading around at every one of Hawthorn's social mixers like a peacock, but that's not my style." I crossed my legs and arms. "I intend to study more often than not, and you know it, too."

"I'm not trying to make you into my mini-me, but you don't understand." His back was to me, so I couldn't see his face. "You can ease back on them eventually, but the social events and mixers that they have these first few weeks aren't optional."

"Mom and Dad never told me that."

"Well, for whatever reason, neither of them bothers much with the grease on the wheels of extrahuman society." He chuckled. "Thank goodness that part of this apple fell farther from their trees."

"Hey!" I stood up, bumping my head but angry enough to ignore it. "You're my brother, so I expect snark and torment from you. But insulting our parents like that is going too far."

"Ugh. No." Noah waved his hand as though shooing a nonexistent fly. "I'm not insulting. Just saying that it's a good thing someone in this family can handle socializing. You should give it a try. Who knows, you might even be halfway decent at it."

I didn't protest. Instead, I left Noah in my room and went to brush my teeth. At least the bathroom had a high ceiling. As annoying as the ceilings were, I'd miss 10-1/2 Hawthorne Street.

I spat into the sink, running the water to rinse my toothbrush. While rinsing my face with water cold enough to feel abrasive, I wondered whether anyone in my family was as over the top as Noah when they were teenagers. He had to get that from somewhere.

Maybe it was Mom's side of the family. She never talked about, let alone to them. Noah and I hadn't found even a hint of her maiden name anywhere in the house, even though magi were better than Ancestry.com at keeping tabs on heritage.

What was curiouser was that we'd heard everything about Bubbe, plus her parents and how they came to Salem from London after World War Two.

I shuffled back into my bedroom, where Noah wrapped a selection of jewelry I barely ever wore in one of his scarves.

"Hey, does it ever bother you that we never see Mom's family?"

He froze, elbows bent and shoulders tense enough to hold the weight of the world.

"Bother?" He went back to his task, the slight tremor in his wrists the only sign this conversation disturbed him. "No. If she doesn't want to talk about them or have them around, that's her business."

"I seem to remember a chat we had a year back, the night before you went off to Hawthorn for your first year." I sat on my bed, shaking my head. "You told me that what you don't know can hurt you. What's different now?"

"You'll understand when we get there."

He tucked the silk-wrapped bundle of accessories into a pocket on the top of the oversized suitcase. I tossed my ragged old sheepskin slippers on top of all the party dresses.

"You've got subzero fashion sense, Aliyah, honestly."

"Haven't you ever heard of hygge, Noah?"

"Yeah, but the Danish aren't known for haute couture." He chuckled, leaning over to add a box containing my one and only pair of shoes with actual heels.

"Usually, Cadence helps me figure out what to wear." I stared at my bare feet. "But, well..."

"Good thing you've got a brother at your school with a decent eye, then." Noah's eyes twinkled. Lotan peeked out from his collar, rising up to bump my brother's earlobe with his nose.

I realized then what I should have figured out on my birthday back at the beginning of the summer. I'd wrapped my entire head and heart up in how badly I'd miss my friends when all the while, my brother had spent an entire year missing me.

"Yeah, that is definitely a good thing." I managed a smile.

Maybe everything would work out.

Downstairs, we had oatmeal. Again. Which I shouldn't have complained about, even though it's totally bland. A plateful of eggs or even a bagel with a super-basic shmear might not have sat well in my nervous stomach. Ember perched on the back of my chair, wrinkling her snout. I tried offering her a few grains of my breakfast, but she turned up her nose. After that, she gazed longingly at an apple in the basket on the counter.

"Really?" I reached toward the fruit, which elicited a series of excited peeps. "Okay, then."

Ember's diet was supposed to be omnivorous, and she'd already had some herring that morning. I snagged the apple and tossed it above my head. She launched herself into the air, chasing it down to spear it with the claws of one foot. As she perched to eat it on one leg at the counter's edge, I remember how I used to shave in the shower last year before I got my fire magic and used that to get rid of unwanted hair.

I glanced through the doorway into the living room, where our suitcases were piled in a stack. At least Noah had brought the most stuff. He probably had at least six pairs of shoes. Noah took his last bite of breakfast and headed to the sink to rinse his dirty dishes.

"Are you almost ready?" Dad cracked his knuckles, glancing at all the luggage.

"Mostly." I shrugged, scraping my spoon around in the bowl of half-eaten oatmeal. "But can't Mom come with us?"

Pregnant was a total understatement for the level of pause in the room after my question. She hadn't gone with Noah on his first day last year, but I'd thought it was because she had to stay home with me.

"Lee, I don't think—" Dad started.

"You know what, Aaron?" Mom stepped out of her office, slinging her handbag across her body. "I'll come along. If only to help with all that." She grinned.

I scarfed down the rest of my oatmeal, finally getting some of my appetite back. My mood improved so much, I even grabbed Mom's and Dad's empty bowls to rinse and load into the dishwasher.

After that, I put my Hawthorn Academy blazer on. It felt odd; not the kind of thing I'd have worn at my old school. Fortunately, the jeggings and tunic I had on underneath were part of my usual wardrobe staples.

As we hefted all the bags, preparing to leave the house and make our way toward Essex Street, my mood improved exponentially.

If only it had lasted.

CHAPTER SIX

Rolling a suitcase should have been easy, especially on a street for pedestrian traffic only. But with cobblestone pavement dating back to the 1600s, not so much.

That was what we did as we tried to find where the entrance to Hawthorn Academy was that day.

The headmaster was supposed to be one in a long line of famously powerful space magi. No, he wasn't an alien, just able to ensure the entire school existed in the space between this world and the faerie realm of the Under.

A lot of the more mundanely educated folks thought there was just a barrier there, like a wall. I guess it was easier to imagine it that way, but it was impractical when you were a magus who needed to pull energy out of or even through that space.

Plenty of schools didn't hide all or even half of their campus like this. Providence Paranormal College was one—those buildings were in plain old mundane space, even the ones with magically restricted access. That was one reason they'd had to deal with so much trouble a couple of years ago.

Hawthorn Academy was bigger on the inside and also safer. The pocket-school model did have one inconvenient feature, however. It was a mundane dead tech zone, along with most of Essex Street. Something about pocket buildings messed with wireless everything. Cell phones, wi-fi, satellite, and data didn't work there. No binge-streaming for the students at good old Hawthorn.

Wired phone lines existed inside the school, but they were for emergencies only. The worst part of all this was being unable to message Izzy and Cadence when I missed them, but I'd gotten a top-secret belated birthday gift from my friends. There was no way I'd be able to use it while looking for the migrating door, though.

It was supposedly for safety reasons that the school entrance moved up, down, and around Essex Street. After the Great Reveal when the entire world found out all the creatures of legend actually existed, people had started poking around, looking for places like Hawthorn.

Thing was, I had it on the best authority that the door had moved around back before Mom's and Dad's days here, too. Bubbe had told me, so I sort of hoped the headmaster just thought it'd be more whim-sical this way.

"Oh no, my shoe!" Noah wailed because a suitcase just scuffed his Oxford. "We've got to stop." He pointed at a storefront across the street.

"Didn't you bring a kit with you?" Dad raised an eyebrow. "For your shoes and all that?"

"Yes, but everyone will see me before I unpack and get a chance to use it." Noah pouted. "Please let me go and see the cobbler?"

"You can get your shoe shined back up as soon as they finish the welcoming ceremony." Mom's always been firm with us, and Noah's tendency toward melodrama was never an excuse.

"But Mom—"

"I don't see Aliyah making a fuss, and she'll be meeting all those people for the first time." Mom sighed, maneuvering my larger suit-case plus one of my brother's. "We don't need to put on airs, not with Bubbe's place in the local community and you being third-generation legacy students."

Noah huffed and puffed and knocked his largest suitcase down. As he bent to stand it back up, Dad pointed ahead and to the left, dragging the third roller behind him.

"Found it."

I looked in that direction and concentrated. The faint tint of blue magic emanated from the alcove next door to the tinker's shop. We all followed Dad, heading in that direction slowly to encourage the suitcases to behave themselves. It was a good thing Mom had come along to help. How she managed those two bags without dropping either of them was beyond me, however.

As we passed the tinker's shop, I had a peek in the window. The place always fascinated me with its collection of magipsychic gadgets. Many of them were imbued and designed so anyone could use them. Because of this, every single item in there sat beside its official certificate of authenticity.

Magic or psychic services and devices always needed a license, at least when sold to the public. Magical animals needed them, too, which meant we saw the certifying board every year. The majority of licenses Bubbe issued came in August and September. That was because most of the magi studying familiar-based magic at Hawthorn had to bring their critters in no later than the first of October.

Not having one by that date meant you'd need to start the alternate program of study or leave school entirely.

I leaned my head to the side and gave Ember an affectionate bump. I was lucky to find her when I did, and not just because, as a fire creature, she was compatible with my magic. Dragonets are some of the rarest familiars out there.

I mean, sure, there were plenty of them around, especially in warmer climates than New England, but they were notoriously picky about who they bonded with. Usually this said something about the magus they chose. A dragonet was a sign I'd take after Mom, whose magic was all brute force. The Morgensterns tended toward finesse, one of the reasons three generations of them had bonded with serpentine Tallin.

Bubbe said dragonets picked either the strongest or the kindest person they could find.

I wasn't certain which of those categories I fell into, but as I stared into the light streaming through the door my brother already walked through, I figured I'd find out. That was half the point of a magical education—discovering your potential.

While heading through the door, I overheard something confusing.

"Are you sure, Angie?" Dad didn't often call Mom by her given name, usually opting for "honey" or some other term of endearment.

"No." Her sigh had more weight than the one she'd spared Noah. "But my setting foot in here can't possibly be an issue after all this time."

"That doesn't mean it won't be, especially after current events." I heard a rustle of fabric. Were they hugging? Why? "You'll be okay?"

"You're with me." Mom sniffled. She was almost never emotional, so why was she crying? "I'll be fine. It's her we ought to worry about. In here. Practically alone."

I stumbled on nothing as they followed me down the hall. There was only one person they could be referring to.

Me.

"Peep." Ember flapped her wings, talons clutched firmly in the fabric of my school blazer.

My familiar kept me from toppling over, but the purring sound of fabric ripping meant she'd also clawed at least six holes in my uniform.

Well, so much for making an impressive entrance.

CHAPTER SEVEN

I followed Noah into the brightly lit lobby. It was hard not to squint as I stepped into the glare. I also had trouble keeping my jaw from dropping.

Even though I'd seen photographs of the inside of Hawthorn Academy, the real thing was totally awe-inspiring. The walls were wood, stained a honey brown hue, and polished to a soft shine. The floors were herringbone hardwood in pristine condition. Noah's soles tapped on the surface like he was performing a soft shoe routine.

From the ceiling hung a chandelier. It wasn't what you'd expect in a place like this, having no crystal teardrops or gilt rods. Instead, it was a wrought iron affair fashioned in the shape of a spider, each leg holding a globe filled with solar magic. The spider's eyes glowed with the same light.

"Check it out, Lee." I forgave Noah's elbow to my rib cage as he pointed out the plaque on the wall.

"Lighting fixtures donated by Morgenstern Magical Creature Care," I read aloud.

"This is why we need to make a good impression," Noah whispered. "It's more than legacy; great-grandpa helped pull the school out of serious trouble when he came over from London."

"I didn't know that."

"Peep." Ember's tail curled around the shoulder opposite the one she stood on.

"Thanks for the hug, girl." I reached up to give her a chin scratch.

"Oh, yeah, familiars are good for that kind of thing." The voice to my right belonged to a girl about six inches shorter than me. Her hair was jet-black and her skin tan, with ruddy accents on her cheeks and lips. She held out her hand. "I'm Grace Dubois, by the way. From Quebec."

"Aliyah." I reached out, and we shook awkwardly because of Ember's weight on my right shoulder and something under her arm. "Uh, Morgenstern. From down the street."

We both had a chuckle over that.

"Don't worry, Lune." Grace finished the handshake, then put her hand on her hip, curling her arm around a rolled-up blanket in some sort of sling. "I won't drop you."

"Is Lune your familiar?"

"Yeah. He's a moon hare." She smiled, smoothing the collar of her blazer, which covered a threadbare flannel shirt. "You're really a Morgenstern?"

"Yes, she is. Just like me." Noah's tone was so icy I almost caught a chill. "Come on, Lee. You ought to meet some of the more well-connected magi here."

Grace giggled so hard she snorted. I instantly liked her because the goofy laugh reminded me of Izzy. As Noah led me away, I turned my head to look back, giving Grace a sympathetic smile before rolling my eyes at my brother. Grace winked back.

"Elanor!" Noah dropped my arm, extending both of his as he rushed toward a statuesque girl with a pink pixie cut.

"Noah, darling!" She reached out and took him by the shoulders, placing an air kiss on either side of his face. She was dressed like a jetsetter, despite the punky hairdo. Her makeup included way too much glitter, but her jewelry was straight out of Tiffany's.

"I can't believe your parents made you work in Vegas all summer."

Noah shook his head, clicking his tongue at what I assumed was his school bestie.

"Well, they couldn't let me traipse around up here for three months." Elanor's laugh was like broken glass tinkling on pavement. "I had to manage the act while they helped Logan train his dragon, of course."

Lotan sat up on Noah's left shoulder, his tongue flicking in and out as his forked tail waved on the right. I recognized that as a serpent greeting, and sure enough, a bird with brilliant plumage fluttered down from a rafter somewhere above to perch on Elanor's shoulder. It warbled at Lotan, then shook its tail feathers, which were pink and orange and yellow.

She had a firebird familiar, the sort that usually partnered with magi in musical or other performance arts. I wondered what kind of talent Elanor had and was about to ask when someone interrupted.

"Hi, I'm Logan." The boy grinning at me was drop-dead gorgeous, like a tall ship in the harbor at sunrise. That was the most stunning thing I could think of besides this fellow.

His shoulders were broad, his waist narrow, and his face could have been chiseled from marble. I realized my mouth was wide open, like a fish's or a frog's, which was kind of gross.

"Um, Aliyah." I stuck my hand out, hoping it didn't remind him of dead fish. It felt awfully clammy when he clasped it.

"Yeah, Noah's sister." His smile showed off teeth impossibly straight and white. "I know."

"You know?" I blinked.

"Elanor talked all summer about how her best friend had a sister my age starting here the same year as me and how we had to meet, of course." He shrugged, smiling again. "And here we are. She never mentioned you had a dragonet familiar, though."

"That's sort of a recent development." My voice came out more monotone than usual. "I just bonded with Ember this summer."

"Ember?" It was his turn to blink. "She's a fire critter? And you actually bonded with her?"

That statement was a bit odd, but I let it pass. Maybe Logan felt nervous and awkward, too.

"Yeah." I turned my head, intending to show her off, but my little friend had burrowed all the way under my collar and behind my hair. "Come on out, girl."

She didn't. Instead, Ember huddled in there. I got the feeling she'd hidden intentionally. I could hardly blame her since she'd probably picked up the jitters from me.

"Huh." Logan peered at the space between my blazer's lapels, or maybe just into space. I finally noticed one flaw—his hands. His fingernails and the cuticles were downright ragged, like he worried at them all the time.

"Um." My face felt as hot as a couple of years ago when I got the flu, except without all the phlegm and puffy eyes and nausea.

"Oh, sorry." Logan's grin was like an obvious backdrop on a movie set. "It's just that I thought I saw some tail there." His face went magenta.

He'd called me tail and then pointed at my chest. I took a step back, totally not used to guys dropping innuendos about me, even by accident. That was when I realized what was off about Logan—besides the social gaffes, I mean.

"So." My lips twisted into something between a smile and a grimace. "Where's your familiar, anyway?"

"That's hardly important." Logan flapped one hand dismissively. His lips went pale and thin, along with most of his face. "I mean, um, he's around—"

"Hey, Aliyah." The person behind me cleared his throat. "Is this guy bothering you?"

"Um, I don't know?" I turned away from blazing hot Logan to find relief in a familiar face—a literal breath of fresh air. "Hi, Dylan."

"Hi, yourself." He wore the school blazer with a black shirt and a green barista's apron. "Haven't seen you in a week. How's things?"

"Oh, the usual nerve-wracking experience of arriving at a new place." My laugh was way too high-pitched. "You know."

"Yeah, all too well." His smile was a soothing balm.

"So, what are you up to, now that the Willows doesn't need summer help anymore?"

"I'm working here ten hours a week." Dylan jerked his thumb toward the hall. "They've got an espresso bar in the main student lounge, and I've got café experience."

"Cool."

"Aliyah, I need to introduce you to someone." Noah tugged my sleeve like a toddler.

"Duty calls, I guess. See you later, Dylan." I let Noah drag me away, hoping it wasn't in the direction of another embarrassing boy.

"Later!" He waved, then turned his back on Logan, who looked like he was about to say something.

"Please don't push me at another dude, Noah." I shook my head. "And you didn't introduce me to Elanor back there, you know."

"Yeah, sorry about that." He shrugged, a gesture I recognized as apologetic only because he's my brother. "This time, it's someone in your grade I haven't met in person either."

"Oh?"

"Yes. We chatted online, and she's also looking to go into extravet- erinary at college. Not a boy." He grinned. "Just someone I think you've got a lot in common with."

"Cool." I took a slow breath, hoping to relax a bit before having to shake another hand.

I couldn't exhale since he was leading me straight toward the last person I wanted to see—Faith Fairbanks. Yes, the girl with the yappy Sha who'd called me a "moronic assistant" last time we met.

"Aliyah, this is—"

"Uh, Noah—" I tried to pull away.

"I've met *her* before." The other girl gave me an icy stare. "And she doesn't look *one bit* like a Morgenstern."

Faith wasn't wrong. I looked like my mom, who was only a Morgenstern by marriage. I had no idea what to say, because I didn't know her maiden name or whether she was from a magical family. All I knew was she used to go here.

"Oh, but she is." The cool, collected voice behind me belonged to my mother—a tone I was used to hearing during her long work conferences through the office door. "I'm Mrs. Morgenstern, Aliyah's mother."

"Is that right?" Faith put a hand on her hip, tilting her head. The Sha inside her handbag flashed a canine grin I wasn't certain I liked. "Because to me, you look an awful lot like a Hopewell."

You know how sometimes in a room full of people, the conversation sort of pauses to the point where everyone can hear a pin drop? Well, that happened right then, at the exact moment Faith dropped that name.

Hopewell. The silence continued, stretching in anticipation of my mom's answer.

Now, where had I heard that name? On television. Finally, my fried brain let me remember.

Richard Hopewell, the extramagus murderer who'd tried to take over both Faerie Courts. My mom was a good person. She couldn't be related to that despicable man from the news. I'd never seen her lose her temper, and couldn't imagine her ever harming another person.

"Noah's totally a Morgenstern, but everyone who takes after the Hopewell family is pure evil," Faith continued. "So, are you one or not?"

"I was a Hopewell, yes. That criminal's sister, in fact. I married after attending this fine institution and stopped associating with my birth family." My mother put her arm around me. "And if you or any other student has an issue with that, I've already arranged for you to take it up with Headmaster Hawkins."

"Mother, you didn't have to make a fuss about—" Noah looked like he was about to take a step backward, but Mom put her other arm around his waist, stopping him.

"Apparently, I do." Her smile could have melted butter.

I thought it was strong, parental, and protective, but almost everyone else in this room took a step back, continued their silence as though they feared her. I couldn't imagine why.

"Come on, Angie." My father held out his arm, elbow crooked. "I believe we've overstayed this particular welcome."

"Yes. I agree." My mother hugged Noah and then me, both somehow warm gestures despite their rapidity. "Remember, we are right around the corner if you need anything."

"Thanks, Mom." I grinned at her, more than a little in awe of how unexpectedly badass she was.

As our parents escorted each other out of the lobby and through the door, it occurred to me that maybe taking after her wasn't such a bad thing.

But the fearful looks on all the faces around me drove home the idea that I might be wrong.

CHAPTER EIGHT

Noah pretty much abandoned me once the door closed behind our parents. There was nothing much to do except stand there with my two ridiculous suitcases. Unless I wanted to start crying.

I totally could have. I'm the niece of a man who tried to kill a pack of students at Providence Paranormal College. What would happen when I graduated and tried applying there? Would they reject me? Maybe the headmistress would spell me into orbit or something.

Legacy magi at a stuffy old private prep school are super-privileged. Noah's rubbed elbows with Fairbankses and their ilk. He didn't seem to care if they all acted like Faith, either.

I felt like a total outsider, and I didn't even have a good reason, like the end of the world or being some kind of foreseen chosen one. Nope. Instead, I was a privileged princess from one family I don't share magic with and another that's flagrantly abused its power.

All my problems were secondhand, with no way to counter them.

I had at least an hour before that required welcome assembly. At least I knew what to do next. The far wall was covered with pneumatic tubes, a way to send messages around the entire pocket-universe campus. I headed toward one of them, then fired up my hand with magical energy to touch it.

It lit up to a brilliant orange-red, and in moments, a slip of paper fluttered down to the little hatch in the plexiglass. The paper sailed into my waiting hand after it opened. I unfolded it and read the directions to my dorm room.

"Cool."

I was talking to nobody, technically. This message system wasn't run by ghosts. Hawthorn Academy didn't employ any psychics, not even a medium. Because it didn't exist in either world, the dead couldn't haunt this campus.

Instead, all the paper and the energy that moved it came from a magus working somewhere in here. So, it was them I thanked, even if they couldn't hear me.

"Thanks."

"Why?" It was Grace. She stood two tubes over, blinking.

"Because I was raised with manners and thanking people is part of that." I shrugged, jostling Ember, who was still tucked under my blazer. "Secret evil extramagus uncle or no."

"Makes sense." She peered at her dorm slip. "Well, it's off to the third floor for me."

"Same here."

"You wouldn't happen to be in 322?"

"That's the place." I sighed, shaking my head. "We're roommates, I guess. Sorry."

"Don't be." Grace grinned. "I should be the one apologizing. You're the one who's going to be stuck staring at a bunch of K-Pop posters, after all. So sorry back, from this here Canadian."

I covered my mouth to stifle the laugh, not wanting to draw any more attention to myself. Grace helped by padding quietly toward the wide set of stairs in the near corner. Once we both stood on the bottom step, she said our floor number, and they started moving upward.

The staircases didn't change positions or become some kind of tricky maze. What kind of monstrous headmaster would want a feature like that in their school? I mean, it was hard enough being away from home for the first time without dealing with something like that.

Of course, I knew all this because Noah and my parents had talked about good old Hawthorn for practically my whole life. But what about Grace? She clearly knew her way around, and her family was all the way in hecking Quebec, for crying out loud.

I kept my shirt on and waited to ask her. We were roommates, so there'd be plenty of time to chat in the future. At least I actually liked Grace.

Hopefully, she liked me too, and this wasn't all some kind of elaborate ploy to ridicule me for "social capital."

"Social what?" Grace stepped off the top stair and then moved aside to let me by.

"Oh." I tittered, hands going clammy. "Um, I have inside versus outside voice problems sometimes."

"Hmm." She nodded. "My cousin's a fire magus. He has that problem too."

"I'd say cool, but it's literally not." I hung my head, and Ember used that gesture as an excuse to headbutt me on the temple.

"You're right." Grace smiled. "Fire. The opposite of cool."

Our chuckles carried us down the hall to room 322, which wasn't far, actually. The doors were all artistically carved from wood with numbers worked into the designs, setting them apart from the plain old stained paneling on the rest of the walls. Grace apparently didn't know everything because she clearly blinked at the flat and unadorned area on the door where the doorknob would be.

"I got this."

I held my hand out, palm toward the small rectangle in the wood. Then I projected my magic energy toward it. There was a click and the door opened, swinging slightly inward.

That feature was one reason Hawthorn Academy will probably never accept mundane students; none of them would be able to get into their rooms. Without the correct type of magical energy, this door would stay shut.

Although I bet all of them responded to Headmaster Hawkins's space magic.

I shook off the paranoid thoughts. Noah said that Hawkins went here when Bubbe got the job after his own father retired. This place wouldn't still be prestigious if the headmaster was a creepazoid. Right?

Pushing through the door activated the magical solar lighting system, a feature I was accustomed to at home. I wasn't used to how ornate the walls were. They were the same wood as the door, with similar baroque carvings.

The walls must have been decorated so extremely to make up for the lack of windows. Not a single bare space existed for Grace to hang her K-Pop posters. Even the lights hung from the ceilings, mini versions of the downstairs chandelier.

"That's the most natural supernatural lighting I've ever seen." Grace strode toward the bed on the left. "Is it cool if I take this one?"

"Sure, go ahead." I grinned, heading toward the identical bed on the right.

She set her bundled familiar down at the foot of the bed and then slipped her arms out of an enormous backpack, a re-purposed hiking rig.

I heaved the larger suitcase up onto my bed, then wheeled the smaller one to the dresser on the right-hand wall. Unloading it was easy, especially with Ember flapping around, opening the drawers for me as I worked.

I zipped the suitcase up before it was completely unpacked, however; Grace didn't need to see that last item rolling around in the bottom. I stowed it under my bed, then got to work on the other suitcase, hanging each piece Noah had chosen on the rail inside the slim wardrobe beside the simple desk. At least the furnishings in here were unassuming enough not to be distracting.

"Ahh." Grace sighed, stretching her arms over her head. She hadn't started unpacking, but I wouldn't judge a person over something like that. "It's so good to be out of that stupid pack. You can come out now, Lune."

The bundle of blankets moved, rustling. Ember sat back on her haunches, looking down from her perch on top of the wardrobe. After a few moments, a whiskered nose emerged. It wriggled rapidly, and then the rest of the moon hare's head shook free.

Lune's fur was mostly gray, with a silvery streak down his back, which was what I'd expected to see, based on Bubbe's books. His ears were long, and he held them at a relaxed angle, which meant Ember's presence didn't alarm him.

This made more sense when he came all the way out of his blankety burrow. He was longer and stronger than my dragonet, outweighing her by at least five pounds. Also, Lune was a full-grown adult moon hare, while Ember was still a juvenile of her species.

When he stretched, I noticed a scar on his left rear flank, and when he took a few exploratory hops around the bed, I noticed his limp.

"He's a handsome fellow." I smiled, crouching by Grace's bed and holding my hand out for Lune to sniff.

"You think?" She sat on the edge of the bed. "Most people find moon hares a bit boring to look at, you know?"

"No, he is." I nodded at him. "Coat's got a healthy sheen, and his ears are nice and straight. He looks strong, too. How long have you two been bonded?"

"He showed up when I was eleven." Grace averted her eyes, then reached out to give Lune an affectionate pat. "I really needed a friend that year, and he pretty much rescued me. Hears trouble coming a mile away." I was about to ask her what kind of trouble, but she changed the subject. "Your dragonet's a real cutie."

"Yeah." I chuckled. "Ember's a lot of fun, but I'm still not sure what she's good at besides breaking awkward silences. I have a lot of those, though, so I'm lucky to have her."

"Well, I haven't heard any since we met." Lune stepped into Grace's lap, edging toward her knees to peer at the floor.

"Um." I winced. "I don't want to womansplain, but—"

"That particular incident wasn't your fault—which was why you wanted to escape, of course."

"All the same, I could have handled it better."

"Not really." Grace helped Lune down from the bed and he loped around, exploring the room. "I mean, she's a Fairbanks. Long line of mostly earth magi and mentalist psychics, and every one of them is a world-class pain in the ass."

"All?" I watched as Ember spiraled down from the wardrobe to the floor, where she followed Lune around, mimicking his movements. "Wait, there are more of them?"

"Oh, yeah. Aunt Mabel told me to watch out for them while I'm here." Grace shook her head. "Steer clear as much as possible."

"There's really more than one?" I blinked.

"Yes. Faith's a middle child. Her older sister's a senior, and her younger sister starts next year."

"Wow."

"How is this a wow moment, exactly?" She reached down to help Lune with an itchy spot on his shoulder, looking up at me out of the corner of her eye.

"Um."

I wasn't sure what to say next because this was more like the sort of conversation Noah would have about someone who's not present to stick up for themselves. Was it right to continue on a sour topic like this? Bubbe always said you attract more bees with honey than vinegar.

But I didn't want to say anything like that to Grace. I had to get along with her all year, regardless of whether she gossiped or not. So, I sat like the proverbial bump on a log, saying and doing nothing. That was at least a familiar enough course of action to feel comfortable.

"You're an oddball, Aliyah Morgenstern." Crap. She did think I was weird.

"I am?"

"Yeah. I mean that in a good way." She peered at the wall above the door, which was carved into a circle with hands and numbers, making a clock. "Anyway, we've got to go to that assembly."

"You're right." I stood, my knees crackling like a bowl of cereal recently introduced to milk. "My brother Noah thought I should wear something fancier."

"You go ahead and put on the dog if you want." Grace flopped back on the bed, throwing her arm over her eyes. "I'm strictly a flannel and jeans kind of gal."

"I totally understand."

Even though Grace practically copied my wardrobe manifesto, I couldn't follow it with her, not with the way I'd embarrassed my brother earlier. Grace unpacked as I put on the outfit Noah had selected this morning for the assembly. And I noticed something.

Grace Dubois didn't seem to own anything but well-worn or threadbare garments.

I'd complained about bringing too much stuff. My roommate seemed to have nothing.

Talk about a disparity.

I had to learn a ton from Grace and quickly because the only way to befriend a person from an entirely different set of circumstances is to stop talking and listen.

CHAPTER NINE

Back down in the lobby, the space was full of chairs except for the far end, where a podium sat waiting for someone to step up and speak. Most of the seats were already taken, which meant Grace and I had to walk all the way down to the front.

Normally in academic settings where I had my pick, I chose the row and column closest to the instructor. Maybe I overachieved a little, which wasn't usually a bad thing with career goals in a medical profession.

Socially, it was a nightmare.

Once again, this was a totally abnormal situation. At any other school, I'd have been perfectly fine with the mean girl hating me, with sauntering in at the last minute, or with sitting in front like the big giant nerd I am. At every other school I'd attended, Izzy and Cadence were with me, and I didn't care what other people thought.

Noah was a whole different animal.

As I settled myself in the front and center chair, a fire grew in my belly, one intent on fueling itself with the idea that my discomfort and shame were Noah's fault.

It would have been easy to blame him. I closed my eyes, trying to banish that thought. It was cruel and went against the way my family always stuck together. Bile rose, and a sour taste coated the back of my tongue. I couldn't do the right thing and let it go.

This wasn't garden-variety sibling rivalry, either.

Before I could process this any further or retreat to relative solitude somewhere to work things through, my escape plans were foiled by the start of the assembly.

A *POP!* along with the rush of displacing air blew my bangs off my forehead. Ember clung more tightly to my shoulder, and beside me, Grace gasped, holding Lune closer.

A chorus of whispered voices followed hers. I managed not to add mine, a testament to my anger and the herculean effort I'd made to hold it in.

A man stood at the podium. He didn't do anything so mundane as walk up to it. No, he used his space magic, something he was clearly proud of. A mirthful grin stretched across his round, dusky-skinned face, which was awfully smooth for a man my grandmother's age. His buzz-cut hair was dark brown, without a hint of gray in it.

Headmaster Hawkins had a sense of humor, and even with the deluge of information from my family, nobody had bothered to tell me this. Or maybe this wasn't Bubbe's old classmate, after all.

"Welcome, students!" He chuckled. The resonant voice carried farther than it should have with mundane acoustics. He was using magic for that, too. "I hope the summer left you refreshed and ready to work hard this year."

"My middle name, practically." It was Dylan's voice, murmuring behind me.

"Some of you have been here and done this in previous years. You were expecting my father, but he went on sabbatical and has left the job to me." That explained why he was Dad's age. He was new to the position that fall.

"I'll try going against the grain and be brief." Hawkins smiled, clearly having fun with this. "Welcome students, old and new. You'll get your room assignments at the pneumatic tubes if you haven't already. Your class schedules will appear on your dorm desks after lunch today, and once you have those, all first-years will report back here with them for an academic campus tour, guided by your home-room instructors."

He stood, gripping both sides of the lectern atop the podium with solid hands. I wasn't sure what he was doing at first but understood when he eventually made eye contact with me.

Not more magic. He locked gazes with each student, remembering us all individually. Headmaster Hawkins wanted to know us by sight even if he didn't have all the names to go with the faces.

I felt the tension in the room ease. Most of it, anyway. When people calmed down, the ambient temperature lowered, and that was the sort of thing a fire magus noticed, especially when she hadn't managed to cool her own hot head.

When he locked gazes with me, it felt eternal, although not in any weird emo way like how it was with Ember in Bubbe's surgery. It felt more like this man saw everywhere I'd been and maybe even some of the places I might go someday. It should have been a profoundly unsettling experience, but it was more a minor annoyance. That might have been because I was still angry about Noah giving me the cold shoulder.

"Peep." The dragonet's tail caressed my cheek, cool and soothing.

"Thanks." I reached up and gave her flank a pat.

Hawkins and I continued staring through this entire exchange. It lasted until the empty chair across the aisle to my right creaked.

"Sorry I'm late." The voice was male and cracked slightly.

He was very late since the headmaster had already clapped his hands and waved us off, dismissing us. This kid had missed the entire assembly.

"You've heard me practice that speech a million times, Harold." Headmaster Hawkins sighed. "Just go and get your room assignment, okay?"

"All right, Dad."

"Did he just say 'dad?'" Grace nudged me in the side.

"Yeah." I turned to look at the headmaster's kid.

Harold Hawkins had dark bronze skin and black hair, but other-wise looked very much like his father—stocky and solid. He was much shorter and on the pudgy side, maybe a year too young to be here. He had a long and furry critter curled up in his lap, and I'd seen one of them before, even though they're pretty rare in New England.

"Wow." I stood, taking three steps to cross the aisle and stop beside the boy. "Is that a Pharaoh's Rat?"

"Yeah, her name's Ningirima, but you can call her Nin for short." His face paled as he stared up at Ember, including her in the conversation. "She's friendly, I promise."

He said that because Pharaoh's Rats hunt dragons, the giant shape-shifting kind. And also dragonets if they're hungry enough.

"This is Ember." I held my arm out, and she sauntered down slowly. "She's way more confident than I am, I promise."

"Okay. And you can call me Hal. Harold's what my folks call me." Hal smiled. His eyes cut to my left, where Grace peeked out from behind me. His entire face lit up. "Oh, wow. You're Grace Dubois. I read your essay!"

"My-my entrance essay?" She blinked. "Um, I thought that was supposed to be, you know, personal?"

"Yeah, and it was really something else." He grinned. "The way you described what it was like living in—"

"Okay, um, thanks and all." Grace's eyes widened, and I felt the waves of near panic coming off her. Her stomach audibly churned. "But—"

"Hey, I think maybe we're all hungry," I interrupted. "I mean, Grace came an awful long way and probably missed breakfast, and I couldn't eat much this morning—nerves and all. So, when do they start serving lunch?"

"Oh, not for another half-hour or so." Hal stood, Nin running up his arm to stretch out along his shoulders like a fur stole. He turned to Grace, making a slight bow. "And I'm sorry about before, going on like that. I can get you a little something right now to make up for it. Do you like apples or bananas?"

"Um, either. Or both?" Grace blinked rapidly a few times.

"Half a moment." His brows furrowed. "Here you go."

A banana appeared in his left hand. A moment later, an apple rested in his right. Lune stood on his haunches and sniffed, his whiskers brushing against the back of Hal's right hand. Grace barked a surprised sound somewhere between alarm and laughter.

"Thanks, half-pint."

Just like that, Elanor sashayed by and snatched the banana out of Hal's hand. She giggled, peeling the fruit as she took a seat a few rows up, next to Noah.

"What the ever-living fu—" Grace's nostrils flared.

"You've still got an apple." Hal extended it toward Grace.

"Thanks, buddy." She shook her head. "But that was bitchy. And you just brushed it off?"

"I'm the headmaster's son." Hal deflated a little. "I've got to be a good example, or families might decide to send their kids to some other school. Anyway, I like being kind. It's practically a counterculture nowadays."

"There's a lot of pressure on some of us, for sure." I nodded. Hal and Grace were at least people I could understand. "Others, not so much." I gestured at Elanor.

She peeled the banana, making eyes at pretty much the entire room. Most of the boys stared, watching and waiting for her to eat it. A handful, including Hal and Elanor's brother Logan, averted their eyes. Even Noah looked on, though with an eye-rolling smirk.

I might have been a total newbie at flirting, dating, and the romantic side of socializing, but I'd been on the internet and watched television. Maybe the boys had some weird sex thing on the brain.

With a wolfish grin, Elanor turned the banana sideways and took an enormous bite out of it, cutting it neatly in half with her teeth. I should have figured she'd do that. Noah had told me a million times that she's gay like him.

The watching boys immediately found something else to look at. Some of them even left the room. Grace rolled her eyes and took an extra-loud bite of her apple.

"She's not into boys," Dylan said as he approached our little cluster. "Heard her chatting up my manager earlier. I mean, she didn't get far because Kayla's twenty and doesn't want to lose her job over inappropriate relations with a student."

"So, you're saying she pulled that whole stunt just to freak everyone out?" Hal shook his head. "I don't get it."

"Probably only likes girls and doesn't want boys bugging her all year." Grace shrugged, her stomach rumbling again. "Okay, obnoxious internal organ, I get it. You need more food." She made quick work of the apple.

"I won't have Elanor's problem," I mumbled, but somehow my three companions all heard me because they let out a chorus of sighs. Well, two of them did, at least.

Dylan blinked. Hal shook his head, a wry grin twisting his full lips. Grace snorted. Clearly, my new friends didn't agree with my self-deprecation. Or they were being nice despite all the sarcasm. Or both. At any rate, I felt a bit better now.

"None of that innocent blinking, pal." I tilted my head to look up at Dylan. "You must have looked in a mirror recently."

"Peep!"

Everyone laughed. Nobody else in the room even noticed because all the students broke into clusters. Ours was the smallest, but at that moment, I didn't care. Bigger wasn't always better. As I introduced Dylan to my two newer friends, I realized something.

The fire in my belly was banked. It wasn't completely gone, but it was manageable now. All I needed to do was avoid another fight with Noah for the rest of the day, and it'd go away.

I hoped.

CHAPTER TEN

"So, you don't have a familiar yet, Dylan?" Hal dipped a piece of bread into his bowl of chicken soup.

"Nope. But don't tell anyone." He shrugged, twirling some noodles on a fork. "Mom wanted me to try bonding with one before I went stateside, but Dad disagreed. Said Customs was hard enough on a magus without bringing a familiar into the mix. By hard, he meant expensive. It's always money with him."

"What is it with your mother?" Grace arched an eyebrow, holding a double cheeseburger in both her hands.

"He's got a tiger mom." I waved a triangle of turkey on rye in his general direction. "That's what you said over the summer, right, Dylan?"

"Pretty much. She's hoping I'll get more interested in what she calls "actual medicine" instead of the extraveterinary kind." He rolled his eyes. "Dad doesn't care as long as it's something lucrative."

"Running this school is lucrative." Hal shook his head. "But I'd prefer not to do it when I'm older."

"Yeah, about that." I put my sandwich down, suddenly not so hungry. "Wasn't it supposed to be your grandfather and not your dad running things this year?"

"Sharp, Aliyah." Hal tapped his nose. "You're right. This is Dad's first year as headmaster and it's super last-minute. I wasn't supposed to start courses here until next year, but so it goes."

"Why?" I leaned forward, listening intently.

"I'm not supposed to talk about it." He glanced up, down, and around.

"Isn't, um..." Grace swallowed the mouthful of burger she'd tried to talk around. "Isn't your dad worried he's not ready?"

"Well, some of the faculty are helping him a lot." He waved his crust of bread at a table of four adults, all wearing staff lanyards. "See that lady professor over there?"

We looked. She was the only woman at the table, with long ash-brown hair in cornrows, light brown skin, and blue eyes. She dressed unconventionally for an academic, sporting a touristy Salem t-shirt over a pair of leggings printed with lightning bolts.

"That's Doctor Susan DeBeer. She came all the way from South Africa to teach at this school. She's been here since right after the Big Reveal. I met her one time before today, but Dad had meetings with her all summer."

"What about that guy?" Dylan jerked his thumb at a slightly built man sitting alone.

That fellow looked to be about my grandma's age. He had more salt than pepper in the hair ringing his bald olive-tone pate. A pair of spectacles was perched on his nose, horn-rimmed in a color that matched the owlish creature perched on his shoulder.

"That's Professor Luciano. Grandpa hired him last year." Hal finished the last of his bread, then reached for another roll from the basket on the table. "He used to teach at Academe Magica in the Italian Alps."

"How stereotypical." Dylan rolled his eyes, leaning in and lowering his voice. "A magic-school professor with an owl familiar."

"That's no owl," Grace whispered.

"You're right, he's a Strix, which means he's got four wings and venom." I leaned forward. "They're Roman, and commonly associated with poison magi."

"An astute assessment to be sure, Miss Hopewell. Hmm, perhaps I've gotten that wrong. It's Miss Morgenstern, yes?" An accompanying basso laugh rumbled like rocks falling. "And you've made one incorrect assumption."

I looked up to find Luciano towering over us. My mouth hung open, and I wasn't alone. We all sat there gawking like a nest full of baby birds.

He'd caught us talking about him and was now throwing insults like a student instead of a teacher. And Dylan had thought an owlish familiar was a horrible stereotype.

"Male Strixes have triangular tufts." He gestured at his familiar's head, drawing our attention to the rounded feathers at the crown, chuckling softly. "As you can see, my companion is female."

"Peep?" Ember fluttered to my other shoulder, craning her neck to get a better look, as if she also wanted to learn about the sexual dimorphism of magical creatures.

"Hoo." The Strix blinked. She was either sleepy or thought dragonets were no big deal. Probably the latter since she didn't bother yawning.

The only course of action was my fallback: what would Bubbe do?

"Well, thanks for the instruction, Professor." I stood carefully so Ember didn't get too unbalanced. "You might already know that I'm Noah Morgenstern's sister, Aliyah. It's good to meet you."

Behind the smile I showed, it felt like being encased in ice because for me, fear was paralyzingly glacial. Professor Luciano walking up like that, despite the chuckle, had me stone-cold scared—which was why I extended my hand anyway.

"It might be nice to meet you, too." The professor didn't shake my hand, only stood there gazing at each of us in turn. "However, I see one of your cohorts is lacking a familiar. Can you tell me why that is, Miss Morgenstern?"

"Well, that's not my story to tell." I looked at Dylan, who'd gone completely still. He'd asked us not to repeat his story. There was no choice but to introduce him, but I managed to give him an out. "This is Dylan Khan. He's from London."

"Customs, Professor." He stood, brushing crumbs off his hands. "You must be aware of how difficult it is to get a magical creature over here on a student visa. I waited instead of seeking one out at home."

"Fortunately, not a matter of concern with an instructor's visa, to be sure." Luciano inclined his head. "And no issue for Miss Dubois and her moon hare."

"I've got dual citizenship, Professor." She cuddled Lune, who was clearly not comfortable under the Strix's gaze. "It's not difficult for me."

"All the same, Mister Khan. I'm sure you're aware that if you have no familiar at the start of your second month here, you'll need to change your focus from Familiar Studies to Preparatory Academia."

Dylan nodded, staring down at his shoes. I would have too, in his place because only a handful of students ever ended up in Preparatory Academia. The only reason they even had an alternate course of study was that someone in the inaugural class had lost their familiar in an accident halfway through their first year.

Hawthorn Academy was all about familiars. It'd suck for Dylan if he didn't find one. As far as I knew, my mom was the only person who'd ever enrolled in Preparatory Academia voluntarily.

"Oi, Lucy. Let them off the hook for now, yeah?" Professor DeBeer came to the rescue. She flipped a long lock of hair off her shoulder, revealing a leather pauldron strapped to it. I wondered why until her familiar fluttered down from a rafter. It was a long-legged bird with stark black and white plumage, one I didn't immediately recognize.

"Kek," the bird said as it perched. I saw why she wore that contraption.

"Those are some serious claws, Professor." I grinned. "What kind of bird is that?"

"You don't already know, Miss Morgenstern?"

"Oh, honestly, Lucy." Professor DeBeer rolled her eyes. "She wouldn't be here if she knew everything."

"It's Luciano, Professor, as we've previously discussed. Remember?" Professor Luciano's hands clenched into fists, but somehow, he managed to look tense and exhausted at the same time.

"Right, right." She waved her hand. "Forgot. Terribly sorry, Professor Luciano. Anyway, this fine fellow is named Hammer and he's an Impundulu, more commonly known as a lightning bird."

"Oh, wow!" Hal popped out of his seat, stars in his eyes. "Professor, could I watch the next time you feed him?"

"Hmm, not so sure on that one." Professor DeBeer shook her head. "Feeding time's pretty gory. I'll have to run that by the headmaster. At any rate, I wanted to discuss lesson plans with this old sod right here, so if you don't mind, we'll just be dragging each other away for now."

She stepped to one side, gesturing away from us with one arm and wagging her eyebrows at Lucciano. He took a deep breath, exhaling slowly as he audibly counted to five. I wasn't sure whether to empathize with him or her at that point.

The four of us watched them go, Nin peeking out from her hiding place in the left side of Hal's jacket.

"The professors are the most confusing part of this place, in my opinion." I shook my head. "At least so far."

"Faith Fairbanks isn't?" Grace raised an eyebrow.

"Nah, just another mean girl." I grinned. "Every school has some of those. What's one more?"

Behind me came the chittering clatter of plastic on tile. Hal's eyes went wide and Dylan turned. I followed suit just in time to recognize Faith as she hurried along the food line and out through the entrance, leaving her dropped tray and all the food that was on it strewn across the floor. Her little Sha scurried after her, yapping.

I looked around, scanning the cafeteria for her mean-girl wannabe hangers-on. They sat with Noah and Elanor, plus one more young woman. This fifth individual bore a striking resemblance to Faith. In fact, I'd have thought it was her if you'd asked me a minute earlier. But I realized the other girl was older and pretty enough to be on a magazine cover. Her hair was a brighter shade of red, too.

It had to be her older sister.

Faith's fair-weather friends were clearly engrossed in whatever the three upperclassmen were saying. It included a heaping pile of pointing and laughing at the mess the unfortunate girl had left behind.

It was only then that I realized Faith had arrived alone, and although she'd surely overheard us talking about her, we weren't her main focus.

Noah's table was, of course.

"This is all wrong." I sighed, feeling my willpower crumble.

I should have felt relief that I wasn't getting picked on by the bullies my brother kept company with, and I did for a moment. But that emotion didn't stick, because I got angry at him for siding with the mean crew. That's not how we were raised.

"Yeah, I think so." Dylan's voice was strained. "But what can we do?"

"I'm going after her." Hal stepped around Grace, looking down at the floor to avoid slipping in the pasta. "Damage control is kind of my responsibility. See you guys later."

"Huh." Grace glanced down at Lune, who thumped the floor three times with his left foot. After that, she stared at the clock on the wall. "We need to go back and get our homeroom assignments, or we'll be late."

"Would you mind getting mine, Grace?"

"Why?" Her eyes widened.

"I want to ask my brother something." My hands clenched. He'd gotten on my last nerve because we'd promised each other years ago that we'd never be bullies. A low growl began near my ear. Ember was riled up too, apparently.

"If that's what you gotta do." She took a step backward. "Come on, Lune, let's go. Talk to you later."

Grace headed for the cafeteria's exit faster than I'd seen her move so far. My nostrils flared as I set my jaw and my resolve. I turned toward Noah's table, about to march over there and give him hell. Dylan's hand on my arm stopped me.

"Aliyah, wait."

"I've got sibling business, Dylan. Don't you have a homeroom assignment to fetch?"

"No." He stepped in front of me, blocking Noah from my view.

"Work-study folks get everything early. Anyway, let me come with you."

"Why? He's being a total tool. I have to get on his case about it."

"Because you're angry. That makes sense, but calling him out won't fix this."

"Maybe it will." I snorted. "Anyway, who died and made you the boss of me?"

"Izzy's alive and well, but last week she asked me to help you anyway." He crossed his arms over his chest. "Take a look over there and tell me he's the real problem—the ringleader—and then I'll let you handle it alone, okay?"

"Yeah, fine. Sure. Whatever." I stepped sideways as Dylan turned. We both had an unobstructed view of the in-crowd's table.

Noah sat back, mouth closed, with his lips pressed into a thin line. Elanor leaned one elbow on the table, her casual posture clearly well-rehearsed. The twins stared, eyes saucer-sized as they hung on every word Faith's sister said.

"So, I told the filthy bloodsucker I'd call the police if he didn't stop chatting up my sister and get lost." Her laugh reminded me of a hyena's.

"What did Faith say to that, Charity?" the twin on the left asked.

"Nothing. Everybody knows you don't make friends with diseased corpses." She wrinkled her nose, pantomiming a dry heave. "Even when you're an undeath magus like she is."

So, the oldest Fairbanks sister was an anti-vampire bigot, which went against practically all the values our family had taught us. And my brother was going along with it.

"Plenty of vampires follow the rules." Noah leaned back in his chair. "My grandmother even knows some who are doctors, helping the sick and dying."

"You know that's just one of the ways they manipulate people into giving them blood, right?" Charity narrowed her eyes. "Because that's all they want—to control the world and spread their disgusting disease."

I knew for sure that wasn't true. I'd met many vampires, living in a touristy place like Salem. They suffered every night of their unlives because the rules people like Charity put in place barely allowed them to survive.

"Ass. You. Me." My brother mumbled our old joke about assumptions under his breath like a mantra he'd practiced countless times.

"What was that, Morgenstern?"

"Nothing." Noah closed his eyes, his Adam's apple bobbing as he swallowed. He only did that when seriously stressed out. I watched all traces of protest die in his eyes once he opened them again.

"Good." Charity's grin was downright wolfish. "You don't want to be on the wrong end of this food chain, so don't make me put you there like I did with Faith and her fleabag Sha."

"What's wrong with her Sha?" One of the twins scratched her head.

"They're drawn to undeath magic." Charity wrinkled her nose. "Ugh."

And just like that, my anger changed its focus.

"You know what, Dylan?" I turned my head, looking at him.

"Hmm?"

"I don't want to kill my brother anymore." I set my jaw. "You're right, he's not the problem."

"Good."

"I'm going to save him from this bitch instead."

"Aliyah—"

Dylan was too slow. Seeing Noah cowed like that gave me wings. In a flash, I was beside the popular crowd's table, looming over them, gunning for bear. Ember extended her wings, hissing at them all.

"Mean people suck." I put my palms flat against the cherry-stained wood, narrowing my eyes.

"And losers get no action." Charity's smirk was light and airy like angel food poison. She rested a raw-silk-clad elbow on the wood. "Your point?"

Elanor's titter was too high-pitched, even for her, and her firebird ducked its head behind hers. Noah blinked, pushing back from the table's edge. Lotan reared up on his shoulder, his warning hiss louder than I'd ever heard it.

The twins guffawed, hands slapping the table. The pigeon familiars on their shoulders flapped, cooing along.

I held out my hand, palm up and cupped, calling flames into it.

Then I inhaled, Ember breathing in tandem. For a moment, it felt like we shared a body, that I had wings, and she was bipedal. The air changed around us, shimmering like summer heat rising off blacktop.

The solar lights in the chandelier above our heads flickered. I almost thought I felt them pulling toward my magic somehow, but that should have been impossible.

"Bailey, put it out," one twin shrieked, pulling her rapidly blistering hand off the table she'd been slapping. The other stood up so fast her chair toppled behind her.

"Shit! Hailey, I can't!"

Ember and I exhaled.

The table and everything on it burst into flame.

Including Charity's shirtsleeves.

From above, the chandelier blasted out an ear-shattering wail, counterpointed with a phrase on repeat.

DANGER: FIRE, LOCATION: CAFETERIA.

"Deluge!" The voice came from my left.

Rain poured down from overhead. The table was still on fire, trays and food charred husks. But Charity's sleeve was out, her flesh unscathed.

A spotted tomcat stood in her lap, back arched and tail straight up. He hissed, sand flying between him and the mean girl. Her familiar's quick thinking and their combined earth magic had saved them from being crispy critters.

I could have killed someone. All because of my temper.

It was raining in the cafeteria. And it was all my fault. I felt horror now instead of rage, but I couldn't stop myself. I still breathed fire, and even though I wanted them to, the flames wouldn't die.

"Pull 'em apart!" Professor DeBeer pointed at my dragonet.

"Yes." It was Professor Luciano behind me. Ember squealed, and I felt her grip on my shoulder loosen before it let go entirely.

"Vacuum!" That was Dylan, behind me. The air spell felt different from his summer cooling conjures. There was an absence along with it, something besides lack of oxygen smothering my magic. Ice cold. But how?

The fire died, and the rain stopped. Also, I couldn't breathe. I put my hands on my throat, trying to gasp, but the air around me just didn't exist. My knees buckled.

"To the infirmary with her." The professor pointed, her lightning bird gliding off her shoulder to lead the way. "Now!"

"Got you." A pair of arms caught under me.

I took a deep breath. The air tasted like burnt everything. My stomach churned and heaved. The supporting hands turned me sideways, lowering me to the floor.

Somehow, I managed to not vomit.

"Get her feet." My other rescuer was Logan. That's right, the kid who was so awkward he accidentally pointed at my boobs. Maybe he conjured the rain.

"On it." Dylan didn't literally lift me by my shoes or socks, thank goodness, but he got my knees.

Together the boys carried me out of the cafeteria, where everything was a blur of carved wood, wrought iron, and sickening self-loathing.

I was still struggling to catch my breath, and my body couldn't handle any more. I passed out.

CHAPTER ELEVEN
INTERLUDE

Harold of Change

I followed Faith Fairbanks because it was my duty.

She was nothing nice, but I couldn't fault her for that. All she knew was shock and snark after growing up Fairbanks, and I knew for sure she'd have it even worse when her little sister Temperance started here next year. So, it was my responsibility to make sure she had a soft place to fall.

I knew loads about the other students here, stuff they'd never have told me themselves. The week before classes started and I moved to this campus between worlds with my overworked father, I asked myself what would Grandma do.

Her example would always guide me, no matter what anyone said about her. And they said an awful lot of terrible things, especially Dad.

That was why I had looked through the files on all the other students in my year. I knew they'd think I didn't belong here. I was almost sixteen, just like all of them, although I looked younger. If things worked out the way I hoped, they'd look past that. Some of them, at least.

Anyway, knowledge is power—and when you had as much as the

people in my family typically did, you used it for the greater good. Hence the whole duty thing.

If only I were typical.

"Faith, wait up." Because my growth got stunted when my magic showed up, I'm on the shorter side, which made me feel like I was running to stand still most times. And the floor next to the window by the dishwashing station was slippery.

"No. Go away."

The sound of clanking plates filled the space between our voices.

"Okay."

My answer worked. She stopped and stared, her shock having the same ultimate effect as kindness would have. People without experience being kind needed to practice it inadvertently sometimes, just to start making good habits. Finally, I caught up and stood beside her.

"What do you mean, okay?" She froze, one heel off the ground, with wide, feral eyes. She could have drowned me in them, and I'd have died happy.

"I'll go away. But for now, I'm a bit out of breath. Give me a minute."

"Whatever." She still didn't move. "It figures the lamest kid at school's the only one who gives a shit."

"Untrue." I shook my head. Keeping my expression flat wasn't easy, but it was the only way someone who's been dissed that hard on her first day by her own sister would believe me. "I had to stop three other people from coming after you too."

"Why?" And just like that, she started coming out the shock. Faith's leg eased, her previously upraised foot now planted on the solid hardwood.

"Because we don't abide bullying." I let the corners of my mouth turn up. "Not even from your ironically named sister."

"Oh." The widening eyes that peered past me and then all around the small corridor told me more than the conversation. She wasn't scared of Charity. Faith was terrified, which confirmed my take on her file.

"Oh?" Sometimes, echoing a person can get them talking. Both my parents said it helped ease a coping mechanism some kids had, ones with more trouble than I had at home.

"Well, what are you going to do about it?"

"I'm the headmaster's son, Faith." I held a hand out. "He listens to me. And everyone here knows it, too."

"You can't be serious. I'm a Fairbanks. I know what everyone here says about my family. What if I sting you while we cross this river? Charity would do it in a heartbeat."

"If how she acts bothers you this much, you understand that the way they treat you isn't the only way to be." I took a deep breath. It'd been short an awful lot since I relied more on my magic, but I couldn't let my mysterious chronic illness bother me now. "You're not a scorpion, and this isn't the Rubicon."

"You're not a historian."

"No. Just another kid trying to be fair, and trying to be a friend."

She mulled that over. It was probably just a handful of seconds, yet it felt like forever. Life-changing moments are always the ones we get stuck in. It couldn't have been easy for her.

Ultimately, our familiars decided things for us. Nin peeked out of my blazer. When Seth noticed her, the back of the tote Faith carried him in swayed from side to side. He was wagging his tail, following up with a whine before he thrust his nose into her hand.

"Are you sure?" I'd have thought she asked the Sha if she weren't looking me right in the eyes.

Finally, I could smile at her because I absolutely was sure about befriending her—even if her gaze almost stole what little breath I had left.

"I chase you on these," I waved a hand at my short, thick legs, "then form an informal debate team next to restaurant trash, and you ask if I'm sure?" I grinned.

"Good point." She tossed her hair over her shoulder. "I've still got no idea why anyone would bother, let alone you. Nobody has before." Her shoulders eased down and back. "But I'm sick of that. The way things have always been."

"I believe it." I nodded. "So let's try something different. Walk back in there with me. Let's hang together."

My hand was out between us all this time, open, like my heart. Dad used to say it was too big. Mom's favorite counter to that was, "Of course, he's a space magus." They both had it right.

"Okay." She reached out, taking my hand. "Nobody wants to hang separately."

Her palm was cool and dry against mine. As her long, elegant fingers curled, intertwining with my short stubby ones, I felt something else. Our magic.

It's not unusual for magi our age to accidentally conjure small amounts of energy in our hands, especially at times of high emotion. But I'd only ever read about it before because I was weak in my magic, even for someone my age. That was par for my course, though, and it would only get worse with time.

Faith was strong in her magic, which was undeath. No wonder people feared her. She probably scared herself, too.

If I truly wanted to help, that'd have to change.

We walked together back toward the cafeteria. She let go, her hand slipping out of mine. I didn't blame her. Nobody wanted to be seen holding hands with the fat kid, but the connection was still there between us like the tether-projection psychics describe as linking them to their bodies when they're out of them.

My heart was full of hope, my head high and confident because I was almost totally sure I could make a difference at school, despite experiencing the most horrible year of my life right before watching Mom go her own way. No, not despite. Because of living through that. I needed to make every one of my moments count, and this was where I had to start.

I was going to help Faith Fairbanks save herself if it was the last thing I did.

"Oh, no." Faith stopped in front of me, her back stiff and her head shaking.

"What's wrong?"

"Look."

I stepped around her to see the half-burnt table in front of me. Paper napkins in sodden heaps dotted its charred surface. Dun-colored sand striped the floor. Clearly, this was the scene of an epic confrontation between an earth magus and a fire magus, with a water magus stepping in.

Charity and Aliyah, then. And probably Logan Pierce, too.

"That Hopewell girl's got no idea who she's messed with here."

"She's a Morgenstern. And maybe she doesn't." I sighed, shaking my head. "But the damage is done. They're enemies for sure now."

The silence stretching between us wasn't uncomfortable. There was tension, a sort I'd never felt before. Surprisingly pleasant, much like Faith.

"What do we do?"

I looked up at her, letting Faith see how she brought a faint smile to my face. Because she said, "We."

"Try hard. Run fast. But mostly, be kind."

"That's it?" She snorted. "Charity wouldn't do that for us."

"We don't have to be kind to her, just provide it as an alternative to everyone else."

"I'm not good at that. Actually, I'm atrocious." She clenched her fists. The remains of her energy lingered in my palm. Curious, that.

"Were you good at swimming right away?" I knew from her file that she'd learned that skill later than most people, and also that it wasn't easy for her. Trauma again.

"No. Okay, I get it."

Faith began walking away, picking her way past the burnt table toward the cafeteria's exit. She moved slowly this time, at least for her. For me, it was a brisk pace.

"Where are you going?"

"Class." She adjusted the strap on her tote. "Keep up, Harold."

Her voice and actions weren't much different than earlier, at least on the surface, but Faith's prickly veneer had started to crack. Maybe, sometime, it'd turn into something she could use when she wanted to, like putting on armor instead of it being her emotional default mode. How did I know this?

Seth turned around in the tote. The little magical canine couldn't stop wagging his tail, his eyes bright as he grinned doggily at me. And that was why I didn't take credit for this change. All I did was get a ball rolling. The Sha would be the one to chase it out into the sunlight. Nin would help more than I could. The other kids' critters, too.

For practitioners of familiar magic, there has always been one more factor in the nature/nurture influence on our personalities, compared with any other extrahumans.

Our companions.

CHAPTER TWELVE
ALIYAH

I woke with my cheek pressed against a flat pillow swathed in pilled jersey fabric that smelled of bleach. My right arm was asleep because I'd been lying on it, and my entire body felt warm and weighed down, so much so that I couldn't immediately sit up.

"Ember?" My next thought was for the dragonet's wellbeing.

"Be still." The voice was a warm tenor, like Izzy's cousin Eduardo but without his accent. "We've got you bundled in a weighted blanket. Your dragonet's perched at the foot of this cot. You need a bit more rest."

"What happened?" As the words slurred out of my mouth, I wished I could swallow them because I remembered it all. "Oh, no. I'm a monster."

"No, just a young and powerful magus with a newfound familiar." A cool hand pressed my forehead. "I'll tell you a secret. You're not the first new student this has happened to. He had a dragonet, too. You remind me of him quite a bit, in fact."

"Who was he?" I cringed, expecting to hear the name "Richard Hopewell." "What happened to him?"

"Someone very special." The voice lowered, like Bubbe's when she was talking about my grandfather. "He grew into his powers, and used them heroically after the Reveal."

I opened my eyes. The man on the stool beside the cot I lay on was pale, with wavy honey-brown hair and a goatee. Amber eyes gazed from behind the round spectacles perched on his unlined face. His thin and bloodless lips tilted up slightly, as though he had resting sympathy face. Or something else.

"Are you a vampire?"

"Nobody's perfect." He shrugged. "I'm also an ice magus, for what it's worth."

Out in Haverhill, Bubbe had a vampire colleague practicing extraveterinary medicine. Salem Hospital also employed several, with a vamp physician on their board of directors. They heard and smelled things wrong with living bodies that even the most powerful magus or psychic couldn't.

I blinked slowly. Vampires weren't allowed to be students here. I knew that already, overheard through years of Mom's conference calls, but apparently, there was no ban on them working here, as long as they were also magi. That wasn't something I'd have considered controversial as recently as yesterday.

"There's no way Hailey or Charity let you take care of them."

"And I didn't." He shook his head. "I'm merely an assistant at this time. But Nurse Smith is almost done with them. He'll be with you shortly."

As I lay there, opening and closing my right hand under the blanket to work the pins and needles out of it, I pondered who this guy was. It took some serious mental and emotional armor for a flammable vampire, even one with ice magic, to remain calm at a time like this.

He was alone in a room with the girl who'd almost burned the cafeteria down—and being so kind. I couldn't have managed a feat like that, so of course, I had to know more about him.

"E. Brown, CNA." I read his badge. "Can I sit up now?"

"Yes." He grinned again, turning down the weighted blanket and giving me a hand up. "By the by, E is for Ezekiel, but students here call me Zeke. They say it sounds cooler, which suits my magical element, I suppose."

"Well, thanks for taking care of me, Zeke." I smoothed my hair, which was messy but not matted, thankfully. "Where's Dylan? And Logan? The boys who brought me here?"

"They both departed to get their class schedules." He nodded at the door. "The one with the dark hair said he'd return right after that."

"That'd be Dylan. He's a good friend." I reached out my left arm toward where Ember perched. "Met him the same day I found her."

"I see."

"Is it going to be a problem?" Ember stretched her wings, as though testing them. She opted for hopping across the bed instead of flying over. "The fact that I missed the tour, I mean?"

"The headmaster will show you around, along with the other students who missed it."

"But isn't Charity Fairbanks an upperclassman?" Ember climbed into my lap and leaned against my stomach, resting her head on my breastbone. I cuddled her, of course.

"That she is. But I speak of her sister." Zeke nodded. "Faith."

There was a knock on the door before I could ask how she ended up missing such a crucial part of orientation. She wasn't with me.

I cleared my throat. "Come in."

The door opened, revealing a short man with a buzz cut wearing blue scrubs covered by an assortment of pockets. His neck was decorated with tattoos, black lines in peaks and whorls like ocean waves. He held up a round-bottomed flask filled with water, positioning it between him and me. The line where the water met the glass wavered slightly, then stilled.

"You're doing much better now, Miss Morgenstern." He waggled the flask in his hand. "I might be able to let you return to regular activities."

"Might?" I raised an eyebrow as Ember lifted her head off my chest.

"Yes." Nurse Smith pulled a stool over, rolling it on casters. "I just need to ask you a few questions."

"Um, can Zeke stay?" I was nervous. No, that's a lie. I was scared half to death that I'd get expelled, and if this was a psych screening, I wanted a witness, even if the only one available was a vampiric nursing assistant.

"Of course." He leaned forward, setting the flask of water on the bedside table. After that, he reached toward his largest pocket. A gleaming blue claw emerged, handing him a notepad with a pen protruding from its spiral top.

"Now, I heard that in the cafeteria, you got into an argument with Charity Fairbanks. How did it start?" The nurse flipped open the pad, pen poised over the empty page.

I took a deep breath, closed my eyes, and let it out. I was a bit hazy on that. I noticed that the water inside the flask rolled slightly like it had its own current.

"Peep." Ember nuzzled my chin, and it all came back to me.

"It started with Faith, actually." I told the nurse she ran off, and how I realized why. I stopped before getting to what I overheard. "Look, I don't want to repeat what she said, even though I sort of have to."

"Why not?"

'Because it's hate speech, Nurse Smith." I glanced at Zeke. "It's also total hogwash, and I don't want to repeat that pack of lies. It's nasty and might hurt someone."

"Like fire might hurt someone?"

Nurse Smith's words hit me like a breaker hitting the shore.

"I didn't mean to shoot the flames out, only conjure them."

"Peep!" Ember had my back, at least.

"Okay." He nodded. "So, was this hate speech against your Jewish heritage? Or perhaps against fire or solar magi?"

"No." I sighed, not looking at Zeke. "It was anti-vampire."

"Hmm." His eyes cut left, then he marked something down on the paper. "Charity told me that you said, 'Mean people suck.' Is that true?"

"Yes."

"And then you set the table on fire?"

"No." I shook my head. "That's not how it happened."

I told him about her insult, how I was pretty much struck speechless. How I wasn't even aware of raising the temperature around me while making the flame in my hand.

"So, it's a simple loss of control, then." Nurse Smith nodded.

"No. It wasn't simple." I swallowed. "I wish it was. But people got hurt, so it's way more complicated."

I left out the part where I felt like Ember and I had merged, and the bit about the lights. That had to be some sort of hallucination because I couldn't do solar magic. I'd have had to be an extramagus to affect those lights or even draw energy from them.

I shook my head again. The esteemed medical professionals might have thought I was trying to remember, not deciding whether to lie, but it was all too much for me to handle or even speak about when it might mean my expulsion. It wasn't even the first day. I said the only thing I could be sure of.

"This was all my fault." My shoulders drooped, and I cradled Ember. "I flew off the handle, and I'm sorry. Should have had better control."

"Miss Morgenstern," Nurse Smith said, patting my arm. "This is actually quite common with fire magi your age."

"Really?"

"Yes. In fact, your own mother struggled the same way when she was a student here." He made another note on his pad. I must have seemed confused because when he glanced up again, he said, "Oh, I see. She hasn't discussed that with you."

"No." I looked up at the clock, unable to meet the nurse's gaze. "All she did was teach me some meditation techniques. But those aren't so helpful now that I'm here. I feel like a total freak."

"You're in an unfamiliar place. It's your first day, and you stood up for what you believe in." Nurse Smith gave me a gentle smile. "It sounds like normal behavior to me."

"This wouldn't have been my kind of normal last year."

"Your magic wasn't as developed then. Remember, you and all the other students here are growing into their powers. It's going to take adjustment on everyone's part."

"Am I expelled?"

"Oh, goodness, no." The nurse tucked his pad and pen back in his pocket. "But I'm afraid you'll have an extra course for this first month of school. It's time-consuming, but it will help you avoid control issues in the future. It's designed for students who aren't fitting in for various reasons."

"What?" I blinked. My plans for afternoons off-campus with Cadence and Izzy would be foiled.

"Headmaster Hawkins will fill you in on all the details during your tour." He picked up the flask, which I'd almost forgotten about, and put that away too. "Now, if you'll excuse me, I need to go and write some reports."

Was he using the flask as some kind of lie detector? No, that was more of an air thing. With water as his element, the nurse probably used it as a way to gauge emotional states.

"Your roommate brought a bag while you were sleeping." Zeke pulled it out from under the bed. "You can freshen up while you wait for the headmaster."

"Wow." I took the bag, setting it on the table beside me. "Thank you, Zeke. For everything."

"It was no trouble." The vampire CNA grinned again, less sadly this time. "I would say I hope to see you again, but I'd prefer it if you stay safe."

"Be sure to come back here if you see heat warping the air again, Miss Morgenstern." Nurse Smith stood. Zeke joined him by the door.

As they stepped toward the exit, I spoke. "Thanks, Nurse Smith." For nothing.

At least I managed to keep my inside voice locked away this time.

They closed the door. Once I changed and freshened up, I exited the infirmary, on my way to take my second chance at a new beginning.

CHAPTER THIRTEEN

I wore the same old leggings and tunic again because that was what Grace had packed. She'd also stuffed my course schedule in the bag, bless her. A scrawl of handwriting told me to meet Professor Hawkins in the main lobby, where we had the welcome assembly.

On arrival, I was relieved to see Hal, Logan, and Dylan. Faith not so much, but I was prepared to give her a second chance.

But the twin I'd injured was there too. Hailey. Or was it Bailey? I wracked my brain because I wanted to go over and apologize, but it was coming up blank.

I froze.

"Peep." Ember twisted her head in front of my face, then knocked some sense into me by headbutting my nose.

"Thanks."

My feet moved again, and I was sure it was Hailey who got hurt now. I kept my eyes fixed on the girl I accidentally injured. More specifically, on the gauze wrapped over her wound, no doubt holding a magical compress in place.

"Hailey, I'm so sorry you got hurt." I looked her in the eye as I continued, "I just couldn't stop the fire I conjured from getting away, and I want to apologize for even using magic back there. I shouldn't have."

"Oh." She blinked, but whether it was from shock or to block tears, I don't know. "Well. Um."

"For Pete's sake, don't hem and haw." Faith snorted. "Accept her apology or not, but pick one before you drive us all batty." Her Sha let out a short bark from the tote slung across her body. "See? Even Seth agrees." The little canine licked her arm.

"Okay. Fine." Hailey tilted her head, her side-ponytail bobbing. "Accepted. But that doesn't mean we're friends. Far from it."

"I don't blame you." I nodded, then headed over toward the boys.

"You okay?" Hal stood, Nin dashing up his arm to twine around his shoulders. "I heard all about what happened in there."

"I screwed up." I shook my head. "And I'm going to make up for it. The nurse set me up with some kind of after-class activity."

"Oh, no way." Logan winced. "Not Familiar Bondage?"

I'd have heard a pin drop if Hailey wasn't snickering into her sleeve.

"What?" Hal scratched his head. Clearly, he'd never checked out Urban Dictionary or been anywhere near Snapchat.

"Logan, buddy." Dylan sighed. "It's 'bonding.' They don't have detention, but the next best thing at good old Hawthorn Academy is called Familiar Bonding. Drop the -age and add -ing."

"I'll bet fifty bucks nobody but the Firestarter over there is required to take it." Faith snorted as she idly patted Seth the Sha.

"Awesomesauce!" Dylan clapped his hands, then held one out. "I'm rich!"

"Fetch, puppy." Faith sighed, snapping her fingers. Seth turned around, his long, straight tail sticking out of the bag as he rummaged in it. He emerged with a crocodile-skin wallet.

"Wait." I shook my head. "Are you being punished because you helped me?" I blinked.

Faith whipped out a fifty, tossing it into the air.

"No." Dylan held out his hand, and the bill see-sawed down to his palm. "It's the coursework for misfit kids. I don't have a familiar, so I don't fit in yet."

"That means you owe me too, Faith." Logan chuckled. "I'm taking it also." He jerked his thumb at his shoulder. "Familiar gone."

"Ugh, dropping adverbs is gauche." Faith wrinkled her nose but paid up anyway. "You're not funny, Logan. Like, ever. Go to the library and check out a joke book or something."

His face fell like one of Bubbe's soufflés. My grandma could bake anything but soufflés. Nobody's perfect.

"Never will be, either," Hailey chimed in. "Ya basic."

"I didn't say that." Faith swallowed. "Just that he's got a lot to learn."

"So do you." Hailey rolled her eyes. "You know what your problem is? You're too nice. And you can hardly call a boy that pretty a charity case."

"Seems to me that all of you need improvement."

We all looked up as the headmaster appeared out of nowhere. I suppose it was a good thing this family of space magi decided to open a prep school instead of an old folks' home because otherwise, they'd give everybody heart attacks. Teleportation is startling on the receiving end.

"Yeah." I took a deep breath. "I'm sorry about the fire in the cafeteria."

"Understood." Headmaster Hawkins nodded.

"Now, all of you missed the tour earlier, so this is the only way I can ensure you won't get lost tomorrow." The headmaster clapped his hands. I got a stomach-turning sense of rapid movement that only lasted a second. "Unfortunately, you can't make up for not meeting the professors who will be advising you during your education here."

"Bummer." Hailey rubbed her eyes, blinking, and I didn't blame her. The lighting was different all of a sudden. "Can we go see the classrooms yet?"

"You're already in one of them." He gestured.

We stared up, down, and all around like turkeys in the rain. The headmaster must have teleported us when he clapped his hands. This classroom was different from the dorms and common areas.

There were a few similarities, of course. The chandeliers were that same spidery wrought iron with solar globes, and the clock was just like the rest of those wooden ones, but it was hung on the wall instead of worked into the decor.

The walls weren't carved wood in here, they were covered with chalkboards. Not the mundane kind. These were magipsychic, which means they generated illustrations to go with what was written on them.

One wall actually had a window. It looked out on the Axelrod walking park behind the Peabody Essex Museum. I could almost see my house from here.

Checking the board at the front, I read a message beside a gorgeous multicolor chalked mural of a beach with a man in a Santa suit sunbathing on it. That had to be what Christmas was like in the southern hemisphere. I chuckled before reading aloud, "Welcome to Professor DeBeer's homeroom."

"Yes." Headmaster Hawkins nodded. "Dylan and Hailey will report here for class in the morning. Please feel free to explore the room and read all the messages left for you by your professor. You other four can follow me across the hall."

We left the classroom, all a bit dismayed that the seemingly fun Susan DeBeers wouldn't be the person we reported to in emergencies or come to when we had questions or concerns. She wouldn't be giving our lectures or running our labs either.

"Don't worry," Hal whispered. "You're not alone."

I nodded, then took the chance to look around the hall.

It was more wood, but bleached and polished instead of stained this time, allowing for a brighter though less warm feeling. It was brisk in there, giving the impression that it was designed for students to hurry through on their way to different places.

When we reached the room across the hall, we found it equipped the same way. However, the chalkboard illustrations were abstract instead of immediately recognizable. The colors and placement exuded a depth that was more intriguing than whimsical.

It was obvious that serious learning went on in here, but never in a boring way. This reminded me immediately of Bubbe. I headed directly to the front, curious to know the name of the person with this oddly comforting teaching style. I was too shocked to read it aloud. Faith did it for me.

"Professor Luciano?"

"Yes." Headmaster Hawkins leaned against the doorframe. "He's excited to have all of you in his homeroom this year."

"Interesting." I turned my back on the headmaster, using my impulse to examine the window in here to cover my disappointment. Outside was the roof of the Bridge Street parking lot.

"I'll be in the hall. You have five minutes."

"I'm not sure I can handle it in here." I glanced at Hal, who gazed out the window with me. "Luciano's tough, by all accounts, and he's in charge of all our academic testing."

"Oh, boy." Logan hung his head. "You're right. Poison owl man probably won't cut us any slack."

"If we stick together and study, we'll get by." Hal gestured at a diagram of different magics and how they interacted with each other. It was straightforward, while still containing new-to-me subject matter. "The way these look, it seems like he'll at least be fair, even if his assignments are challenging."

"Are you sure?" Logan's eyebrows rose. "I mean, I'm not horrible at tests on paper, but labs freak me out."

"So we stick together, like Hal said." Faith elbowed Logan in the ribs. At least we were in agreement. Better together.

The four of us circled the room like restless cats. It was hard to concentrate on reading all the messages, but we managed. Luciano's tone was what I expected—business casual. He'd expect decorum and following the rules, for sure, but all of that was stuff I'd done before.

"We don't spend all day in this room, I hope." Faith leaned against a desk.

"No." Hal pulled his schedule out of a pocket in his blazer, pointing out the blocks. "We'll get broken out in the middle of the day for lunch, library time, and our specials. See?"

"Gym before lunch and Health after." I peered at the paper. "And thank goodness for the library period before we go to Lab."

"Yeah, and Creatives is before Gym. We get to pick what kind of art we make or practice, and we're together with DeBeer's class in one big room."

"Awesome." I was relieved I'd get at least some time with Grace and Dylan during class days. Hal seemed like a good guy, and Logan was mostly harmless. I was still worried about Faith. She was intimidating.

"It's almost time." Faith jerked her chin at the clock. "What's next?"

"Not much." Hal smiled at her. "Dad's just going to show us where the specials are, and then we're done."

"Thanks, losers." She stood and hurried out, contradicting her gratitude by avoiding us like the plague.

"Uh, wow." Logan blinked after Faith. "She's dramatic. I'll just say thanks, I guess. You guys are nice." He grinned, then sauntered out of the room, tossing a wave overhead.

"I don't get it." Hal's frown surprised me. "She didn't talk like that after I followed her."

"She's been a mean girl, Hal." I sighed. "Maybe it's her default mode when people are looking. Old habits—"

"Die hard. I know." He hung his head. "I'm trying to change a few of my own, so I get it. But hope dies hard, too."

"Don't expect much." I chewed my lower lip, wondering whether Hal was one of those angry "nice guys" who think being helpful is money in some sort of twisted romantic bank. But I knew anger when I saw it, and Hal seemed more sad than anything else. Or tired. "Low expectations mean less disappointment later."

"All I wanted was to make some friends here." He winced. "Which is going to take a miracle. It doesn't feel like I fit in."

"Oh?" I blinked. Bubbe always says I ought to be a light in the world. Hal was so amiable I didn't understand how he would have a hard time making friends, but here we were. All I could do was try to help. "Well, you're not alone."

"Yeah. I guess Dylan and Logan not having familiars makes them feel weird too." He fidgeted with the sleeve on his blazer, staring down at the silver buttons. I wondered whether he felt as lonely as me, even with a familiar who clearly loved him and his father in charge of the school.

"Don't forget the gal who set the café on fire." I rolled my eyes. "She's a literal hot mess. I hear she wants to be friends with you, for what it's worth."

"Thanks, Aliyah." He perked up. "It means a lot."

We had a chuckle as we headed out into the hall. Everyone else was there, so Headmaster Hawkins started walking as soon as we emerged. Following him, I thought maybe my second chance just might work out.

If only.

CHAPTER FOURTEEN

The Creatives room was locked, so we didn't get to see inside. Knowing its location was a relief, though, because there was no way I would have found it on my own. Professor Hawkins only told us it was directed study with instruction on request. As we walked on, he spoke.

"For those of you in Familiar Bonding, it meets in the infirmary after the last class block."

"The infirmary?" Logan's chuckle was a little too high-pitched. "Are we sick in the head or something?"

"No." Headmaster Hawkins shook his head. "Nurse Smith has all the knowledge and materials needed, however, and he prefers to assemble where he can handle any medical emergencies."

"Makes sense." I nodded.

The gym was open. In there, the walls were once again wood but stained like the academic hallways. It was interesting how something as simple as wood stain changed the sense of place. Izzy would say there was psychology to it, that certain colors helped the mind focus on different types of tasks. Cadence would disagree and say the decor's purpose was emotional.

I wished they were with me.

Bleachers stood against the walls, folded in on themselves. Unlike the ones at my old school, which were made of metal and plastic, these were wood. It was impossible to tell how they opened, but when I brushed the back of my hand against one, I sensed its magical energy.

Great. I was a barely controlled fire magus in a school made almost entirely out of wood.

"Peep."

Ember used her tail to give me a hug. Somehow, she always knew when I needed one, which reminded me of Bubbe and Mom. If they had gotten through education at Hawthorn Academy with solar and fire magic, I suppose I might make it too.

If only I could keep from burning the school down.

I dismissed the seriously unhealthy thinking and continued to check out the gymnasium. It helped take my mind off the idea that my academic career might literally go up in smoke.

The gym had three carved clocks, a scoreboard that was the second cousin of the chalkboards in the classrooms, and four magic chandeliers. I had to crane my neck to look at them because the ceiling was so high.

There were a handful of students inside, running laps on the track outlined on the hardwood. That was where I got what I thought might be a pleasant surprise.

"Hi, Noah!" I smiled and waved.

My brother ran by, totally ignoring me. Lotan didn't do the usual and wave his tail at me, either, and he was only jogging, not even close to his regular level of exertion when working out at home.

I had thought going to the same school would improve our relationship.

My words to Hal back in the homeroom felt more hollow than a collapsing log. A wave of homesickness washed over me. All I wanted right then was one of those long afternoons at the Willows, a time warp back to summer, before all of this.

Headmaster Hawkins moved on before my brother completed another lap and ignored me again. Thank goodness.

"Health is at the end of the hall closest to the infirmary, and like the Creatives room, it's closed." He spoke as he strode down the hall. "After I show you the way, you ought to prepare for the mixer. You're short on time."

He walked so fast, we all had to hustle to keep up, even me with my awkwardly long legs. A glance at one of the hall clocks told me why. It was late.

I wondered why the space magus wasn't using magic to move us around the school as he had on the way here. I was only momentarily puzzled instead of completely stumped by this. I worked it out quickly.

We needed to see how to get in and out of the academic wing, of course. That would be impossible if he teleported us everywhere during the tour. The corridor with the classrooms was long, but half of the classrooms were locked up and dark, unused. I didn't need to wonder why our class was so small.

Life as an extrahuman wasn't secret anymore. New laws, practices, and opportunities had developed before I was even born. This had led to lots of new freedoms for many of us, especially psychics and magi like me—including freedom of education.

Public schools offered so many more specialized programs for extrahumans than in the years after the Big Reveal. Enough to get average and above students into community and state colleges with majors in using extrahuman skills for careers.

Back in Bubbe's day, psychics and magi learned in secret, while shifters and changelings got pulled from mundane high schools to avoid revealing their true natures by accident. The latter often ended up as dropouts because expensive schools like Hawthorn or Trout and The Academy down in Rhode Island were the only places that could accommodate them. Post-Reveal, parents who couldn't afford to send their kids to any other school were now guaranteed public options.

Of course, legacy students like me and families like Dylan's wanted a shot at the best future for their offspring. So, plenty of us still busted our humps to begin and sustain academic careers at the old traditional schools, but we had become the minority.

There were even homeschool options now, online instruction with seasonal labs held in larger cities like Boston. I did loads of research on those, with the idea of convincing my parents to let me learn that way instead of having to stay on this campus.

Considering the day I'd had, I probably should've pushed that angle further, but it was too late for that. I'd gotten stuck being the hot mess in residence at Hawthorn Academy.

But things could only get better, right? I had to keep on hoping. It was only the first day, so even if I couldn't make up with Noah and fix all the problems, there was always tomorrow. And the day after that. But I wasn't sure how to manage.

My temper was a big problem. A fire magus in a school made almost entirely of wood could never be completely at ease.

I missed Izzy and Cadence in a big way. All I needed to do was get through the next few hours, and hopefully, I'd be able to talk to them without getting caught, because my means to do so was totally against school rules.

The headmaster pushed through a set of doors inlaid with stained glass. The cut and soldered pieces made a pair of pictures, one on each side. The first one showed the bay here in Salem, the sun rising over it in shards of orange, purple, and pink. The other depicted Gallows Hill at night, bare tree branches reaching to touch a full moon, all yellow, blue, and black.

The designs reminded me of the faerie courts, something I didn't expect to be confronted with here at school. There was only one family with fae living in Salem, the Ambersmiths. Which made me wonder who the artist was, and how these pieces came to be here. The act of making that art might have been pure rebellion.

I got so curious about them I stopped, not caring about having to jog to catch up with the group later. Like most other elements of decor here at Hawthorn, these doors had a plaque beside them.

"Long Division," I read. "Created by Gamila Hadaad–Hawkins." I closed my mouth, pondering the name along with the date, which I didn't read aloud.

The stained-glass artwork was about the same age as my new

friend Hal. The fact that the artist shared his last name made me wonder how they were related—by marriage with that hyphen there, perhaps. But there was no way Hal Hawkins was old enough to get married, even with parental consent. Also, that was only a common practice among magical shifters, so Gamila Hadaad-Hawkins must be some other maternal relative. Probably with faerie blood.

The sound behind me practically had me jumping out of my skin. Ember flew off my shoulder, propelling herself upward and emitting a roar instead of her usual peep. I turned on my heel and felt nearly instantaneous relief. It was just the headmaster.

"My mother made that, you know." He nodded at the doors. "She used to oversee Creatives. Do you like it?"

"It's sad, somehow?" And that was true. Something about the scene, its mood, maybe, or the title, nagged at my mind. "But I'm not sure."

"Well, come and see me in class when you decide." He nodded. "I'm in charge of Creatives for your year. But for now, there's a mixer everyone needs to attend."

"I'm sorry about everything." I held out my arm so Ember could land. "It feels like I've done nothing but ruin your day. And a number of other people's too."

"These things happen. What's important is that we don't let the hiccups define our ability to breathe." He shrugged. "Or some analogy more profound than I can come up with."

"You're not anything like I expected, Headmaster." I couldn't keep the smile off my lips without letting the laughter behind it out.

"Well, we can't all be wise bearded sages." He chuckled. "Although with a little luck, some far future class or other at this institution will get the chance to see me that way."

"Do I really have to be at the mixer, Headmaster?"

"Well, at least stay for a half-hour, through the presentation of faces and names." He gave me a sidelong glance. "Unless you're still ill and need to spend the night in the infirmary?"

"No, I'm just tired is all." The last thing I wanted was to get stuck all night away from my room and the contraband object I'd hidden in there. "I'll tough it out."

Instead of leading the way, Headmaster Hawkins walked beside me around the corner that led to the lobby. The place was packed with students and teachers, most of them dressed in cocktail attire. Noah was right—a varied wardrobe was a necessity here.

It seemed like everyone had gotten fancied up. Even Hailey had passable attire for the occasion, which I realized must be because her twin had brought clothes to the infirmary that'd fit her. I searched the room, hoping to find somebody—even one person—as dressed-down as I was.

Across the room, I saw her: Grace, my roommate. She was still clad in the same pegged jeans and threadbare flannel she'd arrived at school this morning wearing, with the school blazer, of course. As I stood in a corner, tugging at the hem of my blazer and hoping it covered the understated tunic atop my leggings, Grace guffawed with Dylan as though she hadn't a care in the world. Hal joined them, adding his quiet and grinning presence to the small group.

If I could have bottled my roommate's confidence and sold it, I'd be a millionaire.

As I considered my newfound lack of bravery, I scanned the room for more folks I'd met on my first day. Faith hovered at the fringes of her sister's group, saying nothing but molding her features into a resting bitch face that might just have had the power to silence Izzy's sass. I realized she must be trying to patch things up with her sibling. I couldn't blame her for trying because I'd made the same effort in the gym with Noah. But Charity was just awful, and I was surprised Faith wasn't trying to escape her orbit.

Until she did.

Logan sauntered through the archway I was standing beside. He saw me and started to head over. I waffled between wincing in anticipation of his social gaffes and relief that someone, *anyone*, noticed me flirting unwillingly with pariah status. At least he was smiling, and the sentiment looked genuine. But he was from a showbiz family, after all. I couldn't decide whether to take his goodwill at face value or consider it a veneer.

Faith intercepted him, hooking her arm around his. He blinked, then furrowed his brow, whispering something to her. She shook her head, giving him a look that'd wilt daisies. The pair of them headed back toward Charity's cluster of beautiful people. I suppose that was best for Logan. He certainly looked like he belonged with them, awkward or not.

I stopped people-watching to look for my brother. He hadn't arrived yet, but Noah loved being fashionably late. Even though he'd snubbed me back in the gym, I wanted to see him.

As I turned myself into a wallflower, leaning near the archway I came in through, I wondered how he did it. Fitting in here, I mean. Everything about this school was opposite to how home felt. Like alien territory, as though I came from another planet.

Hawthorn Academy is technically in another dimension, after all, one Noah's taken to like a duck to water. I watched him saunter in arm-in-arm with his bestie, Elanor. He'd never had a friend who carried on with him like that back at public school, and his entrance wouldn't have gotten such a positive reaction back then, either. People actually stopped, smiling or rushing over to say hello. My brother was Mr. Popularity. Watching his reception and his reaction to it, I understood.

This was Noah's home now. Had been for a year before I got here, and if he was a duck in this water, I was oil on top of it, unable to mix in or blend. Off in the opposite corner, I spotted someone I recognized from pictures Noah had shown me over the summer—Darren, his boyfriend. An introvert. But even he wasn't by himself. Another boy I didn't recognize was over there with him, leaning against the wall.

Suddenly, I couldn't even bear people-watching anymore. I turned my head, resting it against Ember's flank to hide my eyes. I'd wait this mandatory event out and go back to my room.

Because I didn't want anyone to see the tears I couldn't keep in anymore.

Somewhere in the haze of stomach-dropping anguish, I heard the chandelier loudspeaker apparatus announcing names in alphabetical order. That must have been what Headmaster Hawkins meant about faces and names, so I looked up.

A magipsychic display on one wall lighted up. It was like a mundane electronic screen in function, but completely different in how it operated. It was basically a giant HD device with a psychic source and magical power.

Faces of students with their familiars flashed on the screen, along with their names in both text and speech. My stomach felt even worse when I realized the images were generated directly from each person in real-time. The device was taking our pictures right then and there.

And I looked like a waterlogged albatross.

"GRACE DUBOIS: FAMILIAR LUNE," the magically amplified voice said.

As the alphabet moved past F for Fairbanks and on to H for Hawkins, I wiped my eyes on my sleeve. I managed to dab my nose with the hem of my tunic by the time Dylan Khan's face flashed on the screen. I thought I couldn't look too bad until the name Aliyah Morgenstern, familiar Ember boomed through the room.

The face on the screen was blotchy and tearstained, the eyes red-rimmed. And my cowlick stood up in full force, making one side of my hair nearly vertical like Bubbe's yearbook back when New Wave hairstyles were cool. At least Ember looked decent, even if her expression was more feral than usual.

"The new dark lord—"

"Should have said Hopewell—"

"Almost burned the school down—"

Fragments of conversation like shattering mirrors came from red supergiant it-girl Charity and her solar system of mean planets. I hoped she collapsed someday to turn into a supermassive black hole.

They even ignored the boy right after me, a fellow with some sort of serpent familiar.

Logan Pierce saved me, but not in person. His model-perfect mug appeared up on the screen next, and the voices switched to squeals and coos as they decided to fawn over him instead of laughing at me.

And the alphabetical listing went on. Judging by the number of first-year students, we'd have six in each class, which was about average for a magical prep school.

"LEE YOUNG: FAMILIAR SCRATCH" boomed out. A kid with windswept purple bangs over black hair flashed on the screen along with a lop-eared Sumxu cat, and the presentation ended. Finally.

I wanted to run—turn the corner as quickly as possible—but Bubbe always told me that running attracts attention. I took measured steps toward the arch, forcing my breath into a normal pattern instead of the frantic gasps my lungs wanted to take.

Finally, I made it to the stairs, just managing to mumble the number three. When the steps began moving, I knew I had made my escape.

CHAPTER FIFTEEN

"Is this thing on?"

It felt weird, sitting in bed while talking to a glowing glass orb, but I guess it was better than hiding in the corner on the verge of a panic attack. If it worked, I'd be able to vent to my two best friends. Maybe my only real friends in the world.

The device in question was made from a seaglass orb, one of those items frequently found in antique shops all over downtown Salem. Last week, after I bonded with Ember, my friends and I had bought three of them and spent the afternoon enchanting all the orbs together.

Without Dylan. We didn't want to involve him because it was against school rules to bring a device with a connection to the outside world. That seemed unnecessarily cruel, which was why we decided to break the rule, but if Dylan got in trouble for something like this, he'd lose his scholarship and have to go home.

"Testing? One? Two?"

Closing my eyes, I inwardly bemoaned the fact that it would have taken months plus help from an actual telepathic psychic to get the orbs to transmit thoughts instead of speech. That would also have required more education than we had to create. A simple magical voice device was easy at our level of skill.

After opening my eyes again, I stared into its center, only seeing the bottom of my suitcase through it, tinted pink. That came from the glittery substance Cadence had contributed along with her energies. The damn thing was supposed to light up and glow like a candle with an internal flame. That part came from me and my fire magic. And then we were supposed to hear each other's voices through the glass, a feature fueled by Izzy's psychic powers.

We tested it, so the device should have worked here. Maybe I wasn't talking loud enough.

"Izzy? Cadence?" I raised my voice as much as I dared.

"Leelee!" Cadence's voice was a bit muffled, but there, thank goodness.

"Psychics-R-Us, you say 'em, we sooth 'em." I practically saw Izzy's eyebrows waggling as she joked around.

"You guys, I'm so glad this works. You have no idea."

"Rough first day?" Izzy's words were snarky, but her tone was more comfortable than cozy socks in the middle of winter. "I mean, was it bad?

"That's an understatement."

"Peep!"

"Aww." Cadence squealed. "Is that cute little dragony-wagony being a good little girl?"

Ember's tail thumped the headboard in response.

"Yeah, she's behaving way better than me." I hung my head even though my friends couldn't see me. I told them all about my no good, lousy, horrible, rotten day.

I told them everything down to the last detail, including poor Zeke Brown, the vampire CNA who had to live in the school every year with a bunch of bigoted magi. As a matter of fact, I started with him because said bigotry was part of the reason I got into so much trouble in the first place.

"Jeez Louise, Aliyah." Izzy clicked her tongue against her teeth. "That Charity person sounds like a total itch with a B in front."

"What's with the censor bar, Izzy?" Cadence chimed in.

"I'm watching the baby." Izzy means her youngest brother Ricky, who was six, not an infant. But that was what her family called their youngest member. "Gotta watch my language."

"So, how was the Open House at Messing, Izzy? I don't want to be a total time hog." I leaned back against the wall with my open suitcase on my lap. It was the only way I could use the seaglass without Grace seeing it if she walked into the room.

"Not as interesting as your first day at Hawthorn, but I do have a couple of annoying little tag-alongs. They practically followed me onto the wrong bus home."

"You guys are so lucky, going to schools where you don't have to stay overnight and swan around at a bunch of stupid mixers."

"That sounded heinous," said Izzy. "The way they put candid pictures up there without any warning. I mean, who does that to a room full of teenagers?"

"I don't know, Izz." Cadence sighed. "It's hard to remember everyone's name and match them up with their faces on the first day, so I think that's something I'd actually like. But I'm a mermaid, so..."

"Oh, you would have been totally at home in there, Cadence." I groaned. "You've never had a hard time fitting in." I grinned at the mental image of Cadence totally showing Charity's mean girl squad up with her amiable chatter.

"We'll see how that goes when I start my first day tomorrow." I heard Cadence take a puff from her inhaler, which told me she was more nervous than she let on. "It's easy getting along with mundanes, but shifters don't have the best view of mermaids since the Boston Internment. I'll probably hang out with the changelings."

"Well, if things go wrong and you need to talk about it, you know where to go." Izzy snorted. "Under the sea."

We all laughed at the old joke. Cadence gave up protesting years ago that she wasn't allowed anywhere in the ocean besides the shallows in the Bay. Something about her parents' agreement which enabled them to live on land.

"So, are you and Dylan dating yet?" Cadence tittered.

"No, not dating anyone." I cringed, forgetting they couldn't see me. "Nobody would want to, anyway."

"Oh, no." I heard Izzy slap a hand on some surface, imagining her family's kitchen table. "You're not going to get all boy-crazy like our merfriend here, are you, Aliyah?"

"I'm just trying to make friends, not influence people into dating me by mistake." I sighed, leaning my cheek against Ember's flank. "After today, I doubt anyone's interested. Which is good, because I've got too much to worry about right now."

"Speaking of you getting into trouble, maybe we shouldn't press our luck on this little conference call." Cadence was often silly, but any time she said something sensible, she was usually right. "I mean, I'm surprised setting a table on fire didn't get you kicked out, but you're probably on thin ice, so—"

"She's right. It stinks, but I think we ought to get going." Izzy agreed. "Are you coming home this weekend?"

"Yeah, I think so. Unless something else happens. You're the clairvoyant, so maybe you'd know before I do." I couldn't believe I was this unsure of myself, punting a decision this simple at my best friend's extrahuman ability.

"It's in the cards, yeah." Izzy chuckled. "And I foresee Dylan coming out with us for a little while, too. And from what you tell me, I'd like to meet Hal Hawkins, the space magus. Seems like a good guy to know."

"I'll ask." I shrugged. Hearing their voices made it easy to forget they couldn't see me. "Dylan will come out unless he has to work. And Hal, probably. But I can't say for sure until I ask."

"Cool," Cadence said.

"Hey, you guys, thanks." I closed my eyes, the weight of the day's events falling on me as I prepared to end my lifeline call. "I really appreciate you listening to me tonight."

"I'd say any time, but that horrible rule means you have to be careful." I heard the rustle of fabric on Cadence's end. "I'm gonna give you the biggest hug in the world next time I see you."

"Better make that a group hug," Izzy added.

"Thanks again. You're both awesome, talk to you later."

I took my hand off the glass, watching the light inside it fade as the call ended. The entire room felt darker, like it had closed in on me. As I zipped the suitcase shut around my only connection to the world outside Hawthorn Academy, tears rolled down my face. I barely had the presence of mind to tuck the case back under my bed. After that, I flopped back, displacing Ember. As she fluttered to perch on the headboard, I flung my arm across my puffy eyes.

"I wish I was anywhere but here."

I didn't know what I was expecting, but it wasn't my roommate walking in the door as if in response to my statement of misery. I felt my cheeks heat up and immediately took three calming breaths. The last thing I wanted was an embarrassment-induced firestorm right here in my room.

"I'd say that your wish is my command, but I'm no Djinn." Grace held the door open, letting Lune in behind her. "Are you okay?"

"Um." I removed my arm from my face so I could see hers. I expected sympathy at best, pity at worst.

Grace looked like she hadn't slept in days. Lune was even limping, and she had carried him half the day. I sat up immediately.

"That's a question I could also ask you."

"Aren't we like two peas in a pod, then?" She yawned, slurring some of her words.

"Maybe." I shrugged. "But you didn't almost burn down the cafeteria."

"No." Grace rubbed her eyes. When she took her hands away, they looked dull. "It would have been worse than that if I'd lost it."

Grace didn't sit on her bed so much as drop like a sack of potatoes. She pushed her shoes off with her feet, leaving them where they landed. After that, she turned her head toward the dresser, gazing as though it was leagues away.

"Do you want to talk about it?" I tilted my head to one side, trying to figure out if I should call Nurse Smith.

"Not really." Her head bowed like an invisible hand had pushed it down. "Just need darkness. And probably sleep."

"Okay, then. I was about to turn in. Just want to brush my teeth and put on pajamas." I stood. "Can I get you anything?"

"Dunno. Just do your thing. I guess."

I shuffled toward the dresser to grab some clothes, along with my bathroom bag. This was one of the items on the school list, to make using the dormitory restrooms more convenient. I hadn't been in one yet, but Noah had told me plenty over the summer.

"Come on, Ember. I'll be back," I said as I pushed open the door, which wasn't locked from inside. Her lack of response made me pause, staring at the palm-sized rectangle beside the door. "Do you want the lights off?"

"Yeah."

Ember glided toward me and sailed through the door.

I pressed my hand against that smooth surface on the wall and the solar globes went dark. I stepped into the warmly lit hallway and shut the door behind me, leaving my roommate in darkness, probably for the first time today. My familiar landed on my shoulder. Shuffling across the hall to the bathroom gave me a few moments alone with some new thoughts.

Grace hadn't told me what element of magic she has. Based on her bond with Lune the moon hare and her need for darkness, she had to be an umbral magus, but without the affinity that makes some of them totally forgettable. This place was brightly lit all the time with solar magic, and her energy's opposite. Maybe that was the cause of her extreme exhaustion.

Ember fluttered to a perch carved into the row of sinks, clearly there just so flying familiars would have a place to sit. While brushing my teeth, I began to wonder whether we'd both been cursed somehow, or perhaps unwittingly angered a luck-wielding Tanuki. This many unlucky events all at the same time felt like more than coincidence.

Extrahumans don't believe in fate. Magic is more complicated than it seems, and it's got patterns. Over millennia of recorded history, we've discovered that those can be tracked, and we called it coincidence. When the pattern has a net positive outcome, we call it good and try to repeat events, reinforcing the cycle. But when it's net negative, everything's on hard mode.

Maybe I could look for a pattern, something that would help me find a workaround.

After putting my toothbrush away, I washed my face, then headed to the back of the restroom. Ember followed, swooping behind me. Across from the sinks were toilets, of course, making this section look like a hall with plumbing. But past those, the room opened up. Space wasn't a problem here at Hawthorn Academy, so, of course, the bathing and changing areas were luxurious.

The layout was like a Roman bath, with a section for changing and tubs of three different temperatures, plus a steam room and a sauna. Most students wore bathing suits in the tubs because they're communal.

Plain old showers stood across from the changing section, which had curtained cubbies for privacy. I shouldn't have said plain or old. The showers were great, with three heads per stall and beautiful tiles that changed color with water temperature.

I ignored all that, stepping into a cubby with all my stuff. The wall had several hooks plus another perch for flying familiars. There was even a mat under the bench in there for the earthbound variety. Changing into my comfy pajamas and cozy socks was my only goal, so I did that quickly. I'd shower in the morning. Just as I sat on the bench and pulled on one striped fluffy sock, I heard a rustle of fabric followed by a sob. The sound pinned me down.

Who besides me would have come in here to have a cry at this hour?

CHAPTER SIXTEEN

The curtained cubby hid me from whoever was there. I realized this entire situation could turn into another disaster if I reacted without thinking. The girl out there didn't need that so I kept quiet, hoping Ember would do the same.

But of course, she didn't.

If there was one consistent thing about my familiar, it was that she loved rushing in. I reached up, trying to coax her on to my lap so she'd sit nicely instead of flying out there.

Because of our bond, I knew that was what she wanted to do.

On most days, that'd also be my choice. Today, nothing I decided to do went right. I waved, flapped my arms, and made silly faces, but Ember didn't pay attention. She craned her neck, turning one side toward the curtain. I watched her haunches bunch as she prepared to take off.

A moment later, she froze because Faith's Sha Seth whined nearby.

Finally, Ember noticed me and saw something in my posture that undid the tension in hers. The dragonet glided down to my lap, where she let me cradle her in my arms. Arcing her neck up so her mouth was beside my ear, she breathed two times, in and out.

"Peep?" she whispered.

I couldn't respond without being overheard, so I just patted her back, then scratched the ridge between her wings. She trembled, though whether in fear of the Sha or the desire to check on his partner was a mystery to me.

Usually, it was the other way around. Sha feared fire dragonets because fire is the opposite of unliving magic. In ancient lore, the doglike creatures used to seek out desecrated graves, guiding magi with that energy to right the wrongs done to final resting places. During wars between ancient peoples, some undeath magi used their powers to raise dead soldiers right on the battlefield. It was fire magi like me who fought back.

I'd read theories that the soldiers inside the Trojan Horse were in fact the risen thralls of an undeath magus. I'd also read that the very first magus with this power created vampires, but that was widely believed to be pure fabrication.

However, practitioners like Faith were compatible with vampires —not in a romantic way, although that was possible. From what I remembered reading on the subject, even a low-powered undeath magus could draw enough energy from nearby vamps to strengthen their powers exponentially. With a powerful enough undeath magus around, a vampire could go without feeding for months.

No wonder the older Fairbanks girl ostracized her sister. With the right help, Faith could overpower Charity with her hands tied behind her back. A Sha familiar certainly helped with that. Given the bigoted sentiments I'd heard earlier, sibling rivalry could lead down dark paths in the Fairbanks family.

And there I was, getting caught in the middle. Charity probably wanted me constantly on edge, about to fly off the handle because my mere presence in that state would scare her sister into keeping her head down.

My eyes, already sore from crying so much that day, burned again with impending tears.

It wasn't just me and Faith being pushed toward an inevitable conflict. The environment throughout the entire school made Grace sick. Dylan and Logan didn't have familiars but were both enrolled to work with them. Hal was so worried about being here, he had read everyone's entrance essays over the summer. I had no idea what was up with the students in my year who I hadn't met yet.

Why was everything so hard for the new students here? Decks stacked against us on our first day?

As I sat rocking back and forth with Ember, the tears finally came, silently. She hummed softly in my ear, a musical yet mournful sound. It reminded me of recordings I'd heard of dragon-shifter mourning days, the keening they did for hours after one of them died. Maybe in a sense, some part of each of us had gone away. If only the feeling of loss would "move on."

"No, you move." Faith sniffled on the other side of the curtain. "This is my bathroom."

"Oh, no." I held Ember protectively, crossing my arms over her. "That's not what I meant at all. And I'm only putting on pajamas. After that, I'm going to bed."

Seth whined again, much closer this time. I saw his muzzle bump the curtain's hem, pressing it in so it looked like a ghostly doggie nose.

"Well, okay then." Faith's voice came from my left now, meaning she was in the cubby next door. Seth whined louder and longer this time, almost a faint howl. The poor thing sounded almost as miserable as I felt.

Ember craned her head down at Seth's curtain-draped nose, then whispered, still trembling slightly, in my ear.

"Peep." She looked me in the eye, then moved her gaze to my arms and back again. She wanted me to put her down, but I didn't want her getting in a fight with a Sha. I'd have to trust her to do the right thing and avoid a fight.

"Are you sure?"

Ember nodded.

"Okay, then."

I bent at the waist, lowering my arms. And just like that, I let her go.

"Peep?" Ember's voice was louder. In response, Seth's whine took an inquisitive turn.

I hurried up and pulled my other sock on because the last thing two miserable teenagers away from home needed was injured familiars. I stood, turning as fast as I could to sling my bathroom bag over my arm, prepared to scoop Ember up and hustle her out of there. But when I turned back around, she wasn't in the cubby anymore. Pulling back the curtain, I saw the most amazing thing.

My dragonet and Faith's Sha sat quietly together, making small noises and looking for all the world like they were having a chat. Not a cozy one—it was too intense for that. But the sense I got was that they were commiserating.

"Are you seeing what I'm seeing, Morgenstern?"

I turned my head left to find Faith in a near copy of my stance, holding back the curtain in the doorway of her cubby. We stood there, blinking at each other.

"Yeah. Two magi so stressed out that our familiars, who are natural enemies, have to vent to each other."

"I didn't think the first day would be this bad." Faith leaned against the tiled entrance on her cubby. "My sister's a total bitch. What's worse, I think it runs in the family."

"Same here." I sighed. "Except mine's an asshole brother. And ditto on the family thing."

"This doesn't mean we're friends."

"That's not world-ending for me or anything."

"Whatever." She crossed her arms, sniffling again.

"Look, if they can get along, can we maybe have a truce?" I gazed at the unlikely pair of critters as Ember patted Seth's head with the thumb claw on her wing and he headbutted her chest. I know Faith saw that too. "For their sake?"

"Also because our siblings are out to get us, but yeah." Her glare softened as she gazed at her familiar. "For their sake."

"Deal." I stepped out, crossing the tile floor. "Come on, Ember. Let's go to bed and finally end this day."

"Peep!"

She gave Seth one last pat, then sprang up from the floor, heading straight for my shoulder. As I reached the sink and toilet section, the Sha let out a single short bark. It didn't quite cover Faith's voice.

"Thanks."

I didn't look back. Maybe that made me a bad person, but I was about to cry again and wanted to hide it. I echoed the word of gratitude back at her, then opened the door to cross the hall.

When I entered my room, the light tried to come on. Grace's breathing was even and deep enough to tell me she was probably sleeping. But Lune's rear leg moved, thumping near the foot of the bed.

I shut the lights down before they turned all the way up. A fire magus like me will never have trouble getting around in the dark. I called a flame to my hand and used it to light my way.

That one familiar act reminded me that I needed to get a grip as soon as possible. The school wasn't a powder keg, but it was the next best thing. If I ended up igniting it because I'd never bothered to learn temperance and tolerance, I'd be no better than my evil Uncle Richard.

Ember settled in the space between my pillow and the wall. Once she curled up, I extinguished the flame and got into bed. After pushing my feet between the sheets, I turned my back to Grace. I bundled the blanket over the top and back of my head and stared into the dark.

I had no idea how to improve things.

But I could start trying the next day.

CHAPTER SEVENTEEN

Mondays sucked.

The worst thing about them was how, no matter how much purpose and hope I wanted to start the week with, everybody else was going through the motions. Students in the cafeteria milled about, listing from side to side like extras in a zombie movie. We bridged the gap between the end of elementary in sixth grade to prep schools with middle school, which went from seventh through tenth. Magic academies went to thirteenth grade, while Mundanes only did twelve. At any rate, everyone had shuffled through breakfast back then, too.

The morning shamble was universal, probably.

"Peep." From her perch on my shoulder, Ember pointed with one wing at the cereal station.

Rows of containers sat on the counter against the wall, and just looking at them had my stomach growling like a pack of angry werewolves. Somehow, I had forgotten to eat dinner last night. This was why, when the person ahead of me finished shoveling raisin bran into her bowl, I went hog-wild.

If I'd already gotten a reputation as the class weirdo, I'd better have fun with it.

"Ember, go!" I pointed a finger straight ahead, then set my tray down.

"PEEP!" The little dragonet had a big voice when she wanted to use it.

She also had an enormous sense of adventure, which was one reason my little stunt worked beautifully. A mashup of gasps and other expressions of surprise sounded from various points behind me.

Ember pulled off her stunt, a series of divebomb attacks on the most important meal of the day. She got me one scoop from each cereal container, using both feet, deposited them into bowls on my tray, then headed back for more.

I planned ahead for this by covering my tray with as many bowls as it could hold, which was five, incidentally. I didn't care that the cereals got mixed. In fact, that was part of the idea. Some people were corn puff purists. Me, not so much.

Corn, rice, wheat, and oat bits rained down like manna from heaven—if heaven produced cold cereal, that was. I grinned, chuckling softly to myself. Ember had a blast, as well as getting some early morning exercise, but she was clearly done with that by the time the bowls were full.

"Peep." Ember settled back down on my shoulder, stretching out across them so her feet fell to my right and her neck was on my left collarbone. I happily let her rest there; she'd earned it.

"I know, right?" With a wide grin, I picked up my tray and headed for the beverage section to get some kind of non-dairy milk.

On the way, I saw Elanor wagging a finger at her brother Logan.

"You'd better figure it out fast. Mom and Dad are gonna be pissed as hell, and I'm not covering for you anymore."

"Yeah, okay." Logan stared down at the floor.

That made it impossible to catch his eye to see if he needed a rescue, so I continued on my way to the counter with all the drinks and saw another familiar and much friendlier face.

"That was, er, something." Dylan was there, but not for breakfast. He was restocking the coffee urns from a rolling cart, swapping out full insulated containers for the empties. "Are you really going to eat all that?"

'Why not?" I set my tray down and lifted a bowl, holding it under the oat milk dispenser and letting it rip.

"Because it looks good." He reached one hand toward my unconventional breakfast feast. "And I'm a hardworking growing boy, you know."

"Bad magus!" I swatted his hand away. "No biscuit!"

We laughed together. There, so close to the scene of yesterday's drama, that felt like a righteous protest.

"Mondays don't get you two down, apparently." Hal stood nearby, empty glass in hand as he held it up to the juice dispenser. He clicked it off halfway through filling it with orange juice, then moved it to the cranberry. "It's inspiring."

"Thanks, my dude." Dylan smiled.

"When do you get to have a bite?" I waved a hand vaguely at the various food stations.

"After I bring the empties back to Kayley." Dylan heaved the last two full urns off the cart and set them beside the others. "Professors need their coffee because I don't want to risk them dropping letter grades."

"Okay, well, you can sit with us when you get back, then." Hal smiled.

"Awesome. See you in a few shakes." Dylan put the empties on the cart, then pushed it toward the exit.

"Us?" I blinked. "Figured I'd be alone after yesterday."

"No way." Hal set his two-toned juice on his tray, picked it up, and beckoned. "Hawkins family honor code says nobody has to sit alone."

"Oh."

I followed him, passing the roped-off table that still had scorch marks. I shouldn't have looked at it, but it was as compelling as that time a tour bus fell on its side down by the wharf. Disasters were magnets for attention, so, I wasn't surprised when heads turned. My presence might have that effect for a while.

Everybody stared. Even the familiars spared me a glance. I refused to look away, keeping my head up and my eyes open. I owed it to myself to just keep going. Even the biggest disasters were recoverable to some degree with time and effort. If I gave in, I'd be a hot mess for the next three years.

Hal led us to a booth and sat on the outside of the bench. I saw this for the strategic move it was. He knew that random people, whatever their intentions, couldn't sit next to us unless we allowed it. I followed his lead and took a seat on the opposite side.

After I took about twenty bites of cereal, I looked up to find Hal playing with his food. Half his juice was gone, so at least he'd gotten some fuel for the morning. Before speaking, I washed down a mouthful of crunchy goodness with water.

"Aren't you going to eat?"

"Dunno. I'm not that hungry to tell you the truth." Nin poked her sleek head out of Hal's sleeve and deftly snatched a sausage off his plate. Instead of wolfing it down, the Pharaoh's Rat held it up in one paw and pointed it toward her friend's mouth. "Well, I guess my familiar disagrees."

He smiled, cooing at her and patting her head. Then he took a bite of the sausage but passed the rest to his familiar. It occurred to me that in this battle against my reputation and the strictures of magus society, Hal Hawkins was a good ally.

"Do you know what we're supposed to do in there on the first day?" I gestured with my spoon toward the doorway. "In Luciano's homeroom, I mean?"

"Not really." Hal shrugged. "I don't read the curriculum, just watch and listen."

"You don't read, huh?" Grace stood at the side of the table, bearing a plate piled high with home-fried potatoes and a side of ketchup. A smaller plate with something green lurked beside it. "Could've fooled me yesterday."

I moved over to let her sit. As she settled in beside me, Grace left extra space at the end of the bench, patted it, and helped Lune hop up beside her. Picking up her fork, my roommate stabbed some potatoes, then shook her head and set it down. She reached out and picked up the side plate full of carrot tops, leafy green strands trailing off its edges.

"There you go, Lune." She set it down in front of him, then picked up her fork again to dip the home fries in ketchup. "Are you two going to be okay in Luciano's class?"

"Well, at least we're not going it alone." I shrugged, taking another bite of cereal.

"Yeah, but you can't copy off me." Hal chuckled. "You aren't alone either, Grace." Hal waved his nearly unused fork. "Hey, Dylan!"

He slid over to make room for our friend. Dylan had four paper-wrapped packages, which he dropped on the table before sitting. Unwrapping the first, he took a quick bite and chewed, leaning back and closing his eyes like this was the best food in the world.

"I guess I wasn't the only one who was starving this morning." I peered at my five bowls. A few stray oat rings and flakes of bran floated at the edge. My stomach audibly growled.

"Maybe you should go and get more?" Grace lifted her tray, displaying her now-empty plate. "That's what I'm gonna do, anyway."

"In a sec." I began pouring dregs of oat milk from four of the bowls into the fifth. After that, I picked it up and chugged.

"Where do you two put it, honestly?" Hal blinked at our empties. His plate of sausage and cantaloupe was still almost totally intact.

"Oh, yeah, I got a hollow leg." Grace quipped, then moved Lune's now-empty plate back up to her tray as he hopped down to the floor. She got up, grabbing it and moving aside to let me by. "Should have written that in my essay and then you'd have known, yeah?"

"Um." I set my bowl down, exchanged it for a napkin, and dabbed my lips. "Growth spurt this summer."

"Peep!" Ember held her head up, swung it in front of mine, and nodded. She swayed slightly as I stood to move out of the booth.

"Are you sure you're not part-giant?" Hal slouched on the bench, craning his neck up at me.

"Not sure about that kind of thing, really." I stared down into the five empty bowls, reminded of that tarot card Izzy sometimes pulled for me. The Five of Cups, about loss and leaving things behind. "Mom left an awful lot out."

"Oh, crap." Hal sat up, peering past me at something on the other side of the room. "Sorry, didn't mean anything by it."

"Okay." His joke had attracted some unwanted attention, and I was all too glad the excuse of second helpings let me make an escape.

Grace was shorter than me but managed to be faster on our way to drop the empty plates and trays at the dish window. The middle-aged woman who took them nodded. Grace looked her straight in the eye and said thanks, which I echoed.

"Could have been me," she said. "Still might if I don't keep my wits about me here."

"How do you mean?"

We headed toward the pastry and toast counter, where Grace put two slices of bread in the toaster and turned the dial to eleven. I snagged a plate and added a trio of banana-apple mini muffins. There was also apricot rugelach, my favorite, so of course, I took five.

"If Lune hadn't found me at such a young age, I'd be doing a job like that instead of studying here." She snagged a butter knife and stood there, brandishing it at the toaster while she waited. "It's important to count blessings."

"Sounds like something my friend Izzy would say."

"You've got a good friend, then."

"Yeah, known her since kindergarten."

"Is that grade one here?" Grace gathered a heap of jam packets, setting them on the tray beside her plate. "Your schools are different from ours, right?"

"That's the year before what we call first grade."

"Peep?" Ember wasn't trying to agree. When I checked, she was looking down at Lune, who stamped the floor.

"Okay." She wrinkled her nose, then popped the toast early, wincing as she put it on the plate with her bare hands. "I think we need to go back to the table."

We hurried, Grace taking three steps to each of my strides. We must have looked silly, like some scene out of Tolkein with the height difference. But when I came around the corner, all trace of humor faded. Charity stood at our table, flanked by the mean twins. Her cat perched on the edge next to Dylan, whose mouth was full of egg and cheese sandwich. The sandy feline hissed at Nin, who was trying to hide in Hal's blazer.

"Better teleport that deformed rat before it's cat food." Charity sneered.

Hal couldn't. He'd had trouble teleporting fruit the day before. If someone didn't act, Nin could end up in the infirmary or worse.

Fortunately, Bubbe had taught me how to deescalate magical critter confrontations, and my reputation ought to do the trick on Charity too. If I played things right, she might leave us alone for good. At least, that was my plan. But first, I set my tray down on the table.

"Hey!" I put my hands on my hips, standing as tall as I possibly could.

"Oh, look," Charity drawled. "It's the wannabe evil overlord's favorite niece."

Hailey and Bailey tittered, the matching pigeons on their shoulders cooing in counterpoint.

"Yeah." I narrowed my eyes and flared my nostrils, leaning on their expectations to stop them from noticing the tremor in my voice. "Get away from my table. Or else."

"What? You'll burn this one, too? With your little dingleberry stuck in the corner there?" She jerked her thumb at Hal, more than once. After that, Charity tilted her head, dropping a wink at Dylan. "You're too good-looking to get stuck associating with these people, so I'll let you leave if you go quickly."

Dylan's mouth was almost comically full, and he was probably too shocked to swallow half-chewed food. But he shook his head and sat up straight, setting down the remains of his sandwich and placing his hands palm-down on the table.

"Suit yourself, then." Charity put one hand on her hip, leaning into it, and held out another. "Your fire's nothing against my earth magic, little Miss Moldyvort."

I refused to stoop to her level, and I refused to prove her right about my heritage, either. Bubbe had said that kindness is the most powerful magic in the world. I wouldn't become a bully to overcome her. What was it Mom always said?

Justice takes time. Anything instant was only vengeance.

"Ember, go!" I shrugged, concentrating hard on what I wanted my familiar to do. She got the message immediately.

On gilded wings, she swooped down, snagging the sand cat by the scruff, making the swipe she was taking at Nin fall short. Flapping like she was trying to set a record, my dragonet lifted the sputtering feline off the table, high enough to brush against the chandelier.

"How dare you?" Charity growled. "Make that beast put him down this instant!"

"Leave us alone, then." My hands stayed firmly on my hips as they curled into fists. It was the only way to stop myself from flying off the handle again with my magic.

"I do as I please." She smirked. "But if your familiar can't control herself, she'll be put into confinement."

I had nothing to say to that. There was no way I could prove Ember didn't act on her own. Nobody would take my word for it after yesterday, either. Charity was way more experienced at confrontations like this. I shouldn't have tried to out-thinking her. That was why I had no choice.

"Ember, down."

My dragonet flapped, circling until the airsick feline had all four paws on the hardwood floor. At least Ember managed to let the cat go a safe distance away from Hal and Nin.

"You must be such a badass, messing with a bunch of first-year students." Grace stepped up next to me, rolling her eyes. "I mean, really? Don't you seniors have tons of homework plus college entrance exams to worry about?"

"Ugh, the rabbit speaks. Let's go, girls. Leave the future crime-lady and her thug minions alone for now." Charity slapped her hand against the table, letting out a small shower of fine sand. It landed all over our trays and plates, ruining every last morsel of food there, even though it was barely detectible to anyone who didn't see it fall. "This isn't over. I'll make sure everybody here sees your true colors if it's the last thing I do."

With that parting shot, she stalked off, the twins flanking her.

"Well." Dylan finally swallowed the food in his mouth. "This has been a strange repast. But we'll have to hurry to class, or we won't make it in time."

"Yeah." Grace nodded.

"The sand will ruin the dishwashers back there." Hal narrowed his eyes, cheeks going a darker shade. He picked his plate up, dumping its sandy contents on the tray. After that, he repeated the process with the rest of the dishes, stacking them. "Put it all together."

I start helping, getting all of the sand-coated food on the now empty tray. In moments, it was all in a single heap.

"Here goes nothing." Hal put his hands on the pile and stared at it, his brow furrowing. Nin draped herself over his shoulders, letting out a high-pitched trill that gave me the impression she was helping.

Sweat beaded on his temples, forehead, and upper lip. Nin's tail stuck straight up, trembling. The dirt started fading, going pale. Once it was gone, Hal leaned back, gasping like a fish out of water.

None of us knew what to do.

"Oh, shit!" The voice behind me was the last one I expected. "What happened here?"

"Get lost, Faith." Grace rounded on her. "This is your fault."

"No," Hal managed. He couldn't say more, but I understood what he was doing.

Because I was living it.

"Don't blame Faith for something her relative did." I turned to look at the other girl.

Faith's face was pale, one hand pressed against her breastbone and the other outstretched. She only had eyes for Hal. Seth the Sha sat at her feet, looking in the same direction, whining pitifully.

"Get him to the nurse." Dylan got up, moving aside to give Hal room.

"To me?" There was Nurse Smith, striding over.

We all got out of the way, letting the medical professional handle this. He took Hal's vitals, a regular enough course of action, but after that, he got the dreaded emo-detection flask out of his pocket and set it on the table.

"Now tell me," Nurse Smith glanced at me. "Whose fault is this?"

"Mine." Hal shivered like it was below freezing in there.

The water stayed flat. I already knew what that meant.

"Bullshit." Faith leaned over the table, putting her hands on it as though she didn't dare touch Hal but wanted to show support. "We all know who's responsible for this."

"From what I see here, he's being honest." The nurse stowed his flask back in his pocket. "But Hal's coming with me. I refuse to let him go without a full checkup after overextending himself that much."

A bell chimed, signaling five minutes before class started.

"Totally unfair." Faith crossed her arms. "He'll miss his first homeroom."

"Said it was my fault." Hal let Nurse Smith help him off the bench. "Gotta go."

We all watched as they left the cafeteria.

Without another word, we exited, turning toward the hall leading to our first day of classes.

CHAPTER EIGHTEEN

Professor Luciano took attendance. When he got to Hal's name, he looked up and around the room, searching.

"Ah, yes, I remember." He cleared his throat. "Mr. Hawkins is in the infirmary. I've been informed, thanks to Ms. Fairbanks. Moving on."

The first thing he did was give us a pop quiz—ten questions, simple. The only one in the room who seemed to have any trouble with it was Logan. He took the entire ten minutes to finish, occasionally scratching his head and punctuating his many erasures with a series of hems and haws. But he managed to get through it, flipping the paper over and dropping the pencil like comedians drop mics.

When the professor collected the quizzes, he shuffled through them as he walked around the desks. A series of numbers appeared on the board as he checked them over, displaying each of our scores without names to match.

Nobody failed. One person got a perfect score. I was unsure who, but I knew it wasn't me. Another one barely passed, by one correct answer. Judging from my memory of the questions, I was among the nine out of tens.

A lecture on ancient magus society followed, one more interesting than I'd expected. The beginning wasn't about magical creatures, so there was plenty I hadn't heard before. I took notes like almost everybody else. Once again, this was an area Logan seemed deficient in. He listened, head cocked like the RCA dog. He either hadn't heard of taking notes or forgot something to write on. I tore a sheet of paper from my notebook and offered it to him.

"Oh, no, thanks." Logan leaned away from me, not much but enough. Either he bought what the mean girls said, or he had OCD and ripped-out spiral pages freaked him out.

"Are you sure?"

"Ms. Morgenstern, while I appreciate your efforts to assist your classmate, it's unnecessary." Professor Luciano stood in the center of the class, which put him right in line with my desk.

"Taking notes is important, though, and I don't want Logan to—"

"Trust me, he'll get the information he needs." Professor Luciano waved a hand dismissively. "Now, as I was saying, when magi from Rome invaded the British Isles, they discovered an entirely different style of magic being practiced there."

I didn't have to listen to this part of the lecture because I knew it already inside and out. The Pictish people living in what would eventually become the United Kingdom had practiced a form of familiar magic similar to what Hawthorn Academy taught to this day. Being a legacy student was good for something unexpected. I began doodling on the paper absentmindedly.

As I glanced out the window, I noticed that Logan's head was down, his face red. Somehow, I had embarrassed him, but I wasn't sure why or how.

I should've understood from the beginning because my mother dealt with this sort of thing all the time in her job. He had magicpsychic accommodations to help him with lectures, and he probably wanted to keep it a secret.

It was bad enough having people bully me with the whole evil magus angle. Poor Logan had to be just as self-conscious about his unconventional learning style as I was about the Hopewell side of my family.

Professor Luciano moved on in his lecture to a less familiar subject. I took more notes, finally noticing what I'd been drawing earlier.

It was an apple tree, with all the windfalls littering the ground nearby. In defiance, I paused for a moment to draw one more, this time almost all the way at the edge of the paper. "Take that, genetics."

"Is there something you'd like to share with the class, Miss Morgenstern?"

"Um." I peered at the last words I'd jotted on the paper, scrambling for a relevant answer. "I was just wondering what ancient magi thought about genetics. There were so many restrictions back then, more than now, it feels like. I wonder whether people our age had more trouble in that regard than we do today."

"That is an interesting topic, Miss Morgenstern, but a bit digressive." Professor Luciano leaned against his desk and continued, "You'll hear more about extrahuman genetics next year in Health. For now, suffice it to say that the complex social structures of the faerie courts and the coincidental records of magi often prevented paramours from marrying whom they chose. Such remains the case in dragon-shifter families to this day."

He continued to detail how, in magus society, the more things had changed before the Great Reveal, the more things stayed the same. His lecture took us around the world, the magical chalkboards illustrating places and faces to go with the subjects he discussed.

As I wrote my notes, I found myself wishing I could copy all of the chalk illustrations from the lecture as well. The visual references would come in handy while studying, besides being beautiful.

As he ended his lecture, I raised my hand to ask Professor Luciano about getting a copy of the drawings. Faith did the same thing. He ignored both of us but still managed to answer my unspoken question.

"All illustrations are in the books under your seats. You may take these anywhere on campus, but if they leave school grounds, everything in them will be wiped clean." The professor pulled a book from the top of his desk and held it up for us to see.

"This is a copy here." He put it back down. "Incidentally, I have one of these for Mr. Hawkins. If he hasn't returned in time for lab, I will pass this and his notes along to Professor DeBeer, and Mr. Young will bring it to him in the room they share. Homeroom dismissed. Proceed next to Creatives, which you share with the other class."

The sound of paper rustling and bags opening echoed through the room. I stretched in my seat, holding both hands overhead before bringing them down. Ember fluttered off my shoulder, perched on the desk, and mimicked me.

"Um, Aliyah?" Logan stood beside my desk, shuffling his feet and looking at Ember instead of me.

"Logan, I'm sorry. About earlier."

"Oh, that? That's got nothing to do with this." He glanced from side to side. "It's just, can I walk with you to Creatives? I've got a problem."

"I'm happy to help with whatever might be bothering you, Logan." I got up and slung my bag over my shoulder. "Come on, Ember."

The dragonet finished her stretching and took a spin around Logan's head before landing on my shoulder.

"Peep?" Her nostrils flared, and her tongue flickered in and out of her mouth like a snake's. I knew that behavior meant she found something interesting about Logan, but I had no idea what. All the same, I sensed her curiosity.

We headed out of the room together, taking a right to get to the Creatives room. I noticed Faith following Dylan and Grace, who had just exited Professor DeBeer's class. She jogged to catch up with them. There was only one reason I could think of they'd have to leave the academic wing on such a short break.

To visit the infirmary. But I already promised to help Logan. I settled for hollering after them, "Tell Hal I said hi!"

When Dylan turned his head to look back, Faith elbowed him in the ribs and walked faster. Grace caught my eye and shrugged. I shook my head, then nodded at Logan. I'd have to see how Hal was doing later on my own.

"I hope he's back soon." Logan's voice sounded strained. "Hal's nice."

"Oh, me too." I shook my head, sighing. "You probably didn't notice what happened at breakfast."

"All I know is, I saw Charity headed your way, and then Elanor said we should get lost."

"Yeah, it's a good thing you did." I adjusted the strap on my bag. "So, what did you need help with?"

I let him take his time, even slowing down as he decreased our pace to almost a shamble. Whatever was eating Logan, it had to be embarrassing. Finally, he spoke up.

"It's my familiar, Aliyah." He held one of his hands in the other, picking at the cuticle around his thumbnail. Judging by the state it was in, this was a frequent nervous habit.

"Okay." I couldn't think of anything else to say that wouldn't scare Logan out of talking. I felt like I needed to walk on eggshells, but instead of letting it drive me crazy, I just rolled with the distractions.

"So, when I came up here with Elanor last week, we stayed at the Hawthorne Hotel with our folks." His voice was higher-pitched than usual—thready, like it'd snap any second. He picked faster at his thumb, and I worried he'd draw blood.

"Go on."

"Well, I had a familiar with me, the one my parents wanted me to bring to school, and while we were leaving the room one day—"

The bell rang, interrupting him before I could ask a stupid question, which was a good thing, considering I was about to go on a major tangent. How in the world could anyone possibly let their parents pick their familiar? Did all the Pierces think that was a good idea?

And then I remembered—Logan's family was in the business of flashy performing magical creatures. The roundabout explanation of his problem made a warped sort of sense. I should have known. He didn't get along with whatever critter his parents chose.

"Anyway, I was saying," Logan let out a nervous chuckle, "Little guy got out somehow, and I haven't seen him since. He's totally AWOL, and I've got no idea what to do."

"Maybe talking to Headmaster Hawkins would be a good idea."

"Well, that's the thing." He tugged at the skin around his thumb again. "Ow. Um, he'd tell my parents, and they don't know. Elanor doesn't even get how bad it is. She thinks I lost him here on campus. This is such a mess, and I don't know what to do, and your grandmother—"

"Say no more. I'm almost completely sure she can help." I nodded, looking up at him. His eyes were wide, rimmed with red like he'd been about to cry right here in the hall. I looked away. "But I don't get to talk to Bubbe until Friday. Do you think you can hold on until then?"

"I'll try, but yeah, I think so. It helps that Dylan doesn't have a familiar either, so he sort of tanks that aggro for me if you get what I mean." Logan tugged the collar of his expensive distressed t-shirt. "Ugh, my geek's showing."

"That's okay." I put on my best imitation of Captain America. "I get that reference."

Logan made a noise somewhere between a laugh and a sob. Something about Logan Pierce made me nervous, even though he was nowhere near perfect because looks aren't everything. It was like his own anxiety extended around him. All I wanted to do was help him get through it.

Helping someone was fine. I wasn't sure I wanted to date Logan, even though our siblings had tried to push us together before we'd even met, which didn't sit well with me. Neither did the knowledge that his family might be exploiting magical creatures instead of befriending them.

But befriending was what happened there between us, which was nice but not exactly productive. We both forgot a detail so important I couldn't help him without it. We were also almost at the door for Creatives and out of time for this chat.

"Logan?"

"Yeah?"

"What kind of creature is he?" I refused to speak about his runaway critter in the past tense. "Your missing familiar?"

"Oh, yeah." He smacked his hand against his forehead. "He's a drag-onet, sort of like yours but different."

"Okay. Well, what does he look like?"

"I'm not completely sure."

I stopped in the middle of the hall because the idea was so shocking. I couldn't imagine forgetting what Ember looks like, or even Lotan, and that's my brother's familiar, for crying out loud.

"I mean, I can't describe him with words." He hung his head. "Not so good with that."

Logan got accommodations in class for a reason. What would Mom do?

"Maybe you can draw or paint him?"

"Okay, yeah." Logan's face actually lit up. "I love painting, but it does take a while when it's not on a computer."

"You're an artist?" I caught up with him again.

"I wouldn't say that, really." He pulled the classroom door open. "I'm not supposed to be one. But when we're all done with rehearsals and teaching the critters their tricks, it's what I do with my free time."

"Cool!" I smiled. "It's nice to have a hobby like that. I can barely draw a circle."

"It just takes practice." He shrugged. "And you seem smart. I bet you could learn anything. Anyway, thanks for helping me. Thanks for the idea about painting him, too. Never would have thought of that."

We headed inside the Creatives classroom. There were desks like in Homeroom, but also easels with stools. A handful of larger tables stood to one side, some coated in clay and others with precise lines for cutting paper or fabric.

The paneling was more wood, of course, in the light color that was used throughout the academic wing, but in here, the carvings were all rectangular. A girl from the other class had opened one of these panels and peered in, the Sphinx cat beside her looking on with his tail curled into a question mark. Supply closets, of course, built right into the walls.

"Wow." Logan clapped his hands. "This is the best place ever!"

I chuckled; I couldn't help it. His joy was infectious, and he might have been right about it being the best place at school so far. I found a cubby to stow my bag, then began walking toward a desk. But I stopped.

"Let's live a little, Ember." I held out one hand. "Pick a spot."

"Peep!"

She fluttered off my shoulder, doing a couple of circles around the massive room. She was so fast it only took a few breaths. Eventually, she landed on one of the clay tables, an odd choice, but I couldn't complain after leaving the decision up to her. Once I got there, I turned around to see that someone followed me.

"Hey." It was a boy from the other class. I remembered him from the mixer—Lee Young.

"Hi there." I sat on one of the stools by the table's side.

"Do you sculpt the clay or throw pottery?"

"Not sure. There's a first time for everything, I guess."

"Ah." Lee grinned. "Come on, Scratch." He patted the table.

A creature straight out of legend leaped up, sitting up as it peered at me, showing off a stretch of velvety white belly fur. It had floppy, folded ears that were pointed like a cat's, except larger. Those ears were as big as a dwarf lop rabbit's. This animal's haunches made it sit more like a squirrel or a rabbit than a cat.

"Wow." I blinked, watching as Scratch wiggled his nose at me. "Is your familiar a Sumxu?"

"That she is." Lee reached out, rubbing her chin. Scratch stretched out on the table, lying on her side. A bushy tail extended behind her, and I saw that the fur on her back had changed color to match the surface beneath her.

"I've never seen one before."

"Most people haven't." He laughed. "They're experts at hiding and native to my part of China."

"Hello, Aliyah." Hal approached the table. He still looked pale, but he wasn't shaky anymore.

"Hal, you okay?"

"Wouldn't be here if I wasn't." His smile was faint but there. "So, I see you met my roommate."

"Yeah. I guess we're all working with clay today." I grinned. "Totally new for me."

"It's fun." Hal's smile broadened. "Nin loves it. Lee's done some of this back home, too, so you can learn from both of us."

"That sounds awesome."

"Why'd you pick this, anyway?" He gestured around the room, where I saw Dylan carrying an armload of paints and Grace sorting through bolts of fabric like they were the most amazing things in the world. Faith had a sketchpad at one of the desks. "You could have gone anywhere."

"I let Ember decide."

"Peep." She'd folded her wings and was playing with Nin, some kind of game where they took turns jumping. Scratch bounced up to join them.

"By the way, when do we start?"

"Anytime." Hal waved at a man at the front of the classroom. He grinned, waving back. "Dad's busy, so he sent in Master Rosso. He's just here to answer questions and show us where stuff is. Otherwise, it's a free period."

"This is great." Lee smiled. "So, let's make something!"

We spent one hundred minutes working with clay, and ten on either side of that span gathering supplies and cleaning them up. All three of our familiars had a blast, and at the end, we each had something to set on the drying rack.

Hal's pot was pretty much perfect, Lee's was a little taller than he'd intended but still symmetrical, while I gave up on the wheel entirely. I figured my time was better spent making a pendant with Ember's paw print in it plus a handful of beads to match. It was fun to sculpt.

As I washed my hands at the sink, Logan headed over with a container of gray water and a set of watercolor pencils. We rinsed together.

"It's not done." He jerked his chin at the painting. "But it will be in a few more days."

At first, I was speechless. The sketch he'd made on the canvas was already impressively engaging. I almost sensed this dragonet's preening personality from what Logan had hashed out of his face. The artist stood there motionless, probably wondering what I thought because his considerable talent had been largely ignored by his family.

"Wow," I managed. "I mean, that is really amazing work, and it'll be done ahead of the weekend."

"Yeah." He set the empty cup on a rack, the pencils alongside it. "Hey, do you remember where we go next?"

"Gym."

He thanked me. Once we all gathered our things, it was time to head out.

Even though I hadn't been very interested in making art before, Creatives was something to look forward to. Being able to think in a different way and doing a hands-on activity helped refresh my mind.

But Gym was a totally different can of worms.

ACTING IN KINDNESS

The story continues with *Acting In Kindness*, coming soon to Amazon and Kindle Unlimited

AUTHOR NOTES

Hello, readers!

I'm so excited to bring you this series, Hawthorn Academy. It's been a couple of years since finishing the last book in *Providence Paranormal College*, but I knew there were still plenty of stories left to tell in that world. This is one of them.

Hawthorn takes place in Salem, Massachusetts, where I lived for a number of years. Writing in the PPC version of that locale has been a fun and engaging experience. Lots of little details come straight out of my time there.

I actually lived at 10 1/2 Hawthorne Street. The real-life building doesn't have an Extraveterinary office on the first floor, but otherwise, many of the details about it are based in reality. You can walk by the driveway and look up at the building, on the side of the street across from the Boys and Girls Club. But please don't disturb the residents.

The Witch's Brew isn't a real place in downtown Salem, although I designed it to look and feel a lot like the Front Street Cafe with more magic. I've spent many an afternoon there, writing poems and drinking coffee or tea. The biscotti and sandwiches there are delicious, so stop in if you're ever in Salem.

Aliyah Morgenstern is Jewish, like me. Part of the reason I wrote her that way comes from having read the *All of a Kind Family* series by Sydney Taylor when I was young. Finding representation like that is part of what inspired me to be an author. I'm paying it forward. While I only detail Yom Kippur and Passover in Year One, expect to see Hanukkah, Purim, and Sukkot in the next two volumes.

Finally, Hawthorn Academy is a school for magi only. I mention Messing Prep and Gallows Hill, schools for other types of extrahumans. Perhaps I'll write about those in the future if that's something readers express interest in.

You can contact me via my website, drperryauthor.com. From there, you can also find more information about the Providence Paranormal world, other series and books I've written, and links to my social media and Patreon.

I hope you have as much fun reading about Aliyah's adventures as I had writing them. Who am I kidding? I hope you enjoy them even more!

Thanks so much,

D.R. Perry

GLOSSARY

People

- **Changeling**- A mortal child of either one or two faerie parents. Most changelings choose a monarch sometime in their twenties, although some do it earlier than they have to.
- **Dampyr**- The mortal offspring of two vampires. They aren't as rare as many suspect, although because their blood is exceptionally sustaining to vampires, they keep their status secret. Dampyr sometimes have magic or psychic powers that work unreliably.
- **Faerie**- A term used to describe either a changeling who has tithed to a monarch and spent a year and a day in the Under or the pure creatures such as Gnomes and Pixies who were created by the king and queen.
- **Ghost**- A dead person with unfinished business becomes a ghost. If a mortal makes a contract before death, that gives them unfinished business and lets them linger. When ghosts finish their business, they move on, but no one knows where they go from here.
- **Magus**- A mortal who can use magic. Magic comes from

energy in the world. Most magi can only use one type of magic. However, a rare few can do more than one kind. Those are called extramagi.

- **Merfolk**- People who can live on land with legs or in the sea with fins and tails. They only emerged from the ocean after the Big Reveal and are still extremely rare outside of harbor towns.
- **Psychic**- A mortal with psychic power. Psychic ability comes from a person's own body and mind.
- **Vampire**- An unliving person who drinks blood to survive and enhance their abilities. Only regular mortals, psychics, and magi can get turned into vampires. Shifters, changelings, and faeries won't turn, and most of those won't survive an attempt.
- **Shifter**- A mortal who can take an animal's shape. Shifters have one form, with coloring similar to what they have while human. They usually have an enhanced sense while human-shaped, which goes along with their animal. For example, an owl shifter might have keen eyesight and a wolf shifter, a great sense of smell.

Shifter Varieties

- **Dragon**- The only shifters who can see both magic and psychic abilities, though only while shifted. The most powerful ones can partially shapeshift. Dragons are immortal and reproduce infrequently. There are so few of them since the Reveal that they've started taking other magical shifters as mates.
- **Kelpie**- A magical shifter who gets their abilities from an enchanted faerie pelt that bonds with their soul. The Kelpie pelts were created by the Goblin King, so they have Unseelie energy and restrictions. A Kelpie's animal form is a horse. Families pass the pelts down through generations,

and part of each ancestor lives on to help their descendants. The ancestors can get distracting, however.

- **Selkie**- A magical shifter who gets their abilities from an enchanted faerie pelt that bonds with their soul. The Selkie pelts were created by the Sidhe queen, so they have Seelie energy and restrictions. A Selkie's animal form is a seal or sometimes a sea otter. They can use water magic as long as they wear the pelt. Families pass the pelts down through the generations, and part of each ancestor lives on to help their descendants. The ancestors can get distracting, however.
- **Tanuki**- A magical shifter with enhanced speed and the ability to see all types of magic while shifted. They are also the only creatures who can manipulate luck, causing it to turn from good to bad or the other way around. They stop aging if they own a charm infused with luck from humans. Very few of those charms exist, having been either used up during the Reveal or locked away.

Powers

- **Air magic**- The power to conjure, control, and banish wind or air.
- **Earth magic**- The power to conjure, control, and banish earth, sand, or rock.
- **Empathy**- A psychic power to sense and influence emotions in other people.
- **Fire magic**- The power to conjure, control, and banish flames.
- **Ice magic**- The power to conjure, control, and banish ice.
- **Lightning magic**- The power to conjure, control, and banish lightning.
- **Poison magic**- The power to conjure, control, and banish poison. Each magus has a slightly different type of toxin they produce. Some are even antidotes to others.
- **Precognitive**- A psychic power to foretell future events.

- **Spectral magic**- the power to conjure, control, and banish light.
- **Spectral Affinity**- A trait some spectral magi have that makes them charismatic and believable.
- **Summoner**- A psychic power that lets the user make contracts with pure faeries, letting the summoner call them in times of need. Each creature has an anchor, some item symbolizing the bond. Mastery of summoning takes decades of study, which is why the most powerful are either vampires or past middle age.
- **Seelie**- The Sidhe queen's court. The Seelie way is about following the letter of the law, even when it's hard or cruel. They have a hard time reconciling faerie rules with the new mortal laws since the Big Reveal.
- **Solar Magic**- The power to conjure, control, or banish sunlight. Some of the most powerful practitioners can find hidden objects or discover long-kept secrets.
- **Solar Affinity**- A trait some solar magi have that makes them beacons for coincidence.
- **Space magic**- The power to move the self or objects instantly across distances. Some can even move other people.
- **Space Affinity**- This space power comes with an ability to locate people or things important to the magus.
- **Telekinesis**- A psychic power that moves objects.
- **Telepathy**- A psychic power to read minds.
- **Tithe**- The process of pledging to either the queen or king, making a changeling choose to be either Seelie or Unseelie.
- **Umbral magic**- The power to conjure, control, and banish shadows and veil or camouflage objects or people.
- **Umbral Affinity**- A trait some umbral magi have that makes them difficult to remember without psychic ability, faerie magic, or a shifter pack bond.
- **Undeath magic**- The power to conjure, control, and banish unliving energy.

- **Unseelie**- The Goblin king's court. The Unseelies bend the rules and often navigate mortal society more easily than their Seelie counterparts.
- **Water magic**- The power to conjure, banish, and control water.
- **Wood magic**- The power to conjure, banish, and control wood. It takes extreme power to influencing a living plant.

Creatures

- **Basilisk**- A venomous serpent that also has poison magic.
- **Dragonet**- A tiny dragon-like creature, always associated with one or more element which powers their breath attacks later in life. They have scales but are warm-blooded like birds. Most don't get much bigger than a small cat.
- **Familiar**- A magical or mythical creature who makes a bond with a magus.
- **Gryphon**- A chimera which has the head of a bird and hindquarters of a predatory mammal. They come in several combinations of base species, and habitat influences their choice in magi to bond with.
- **Karkus**- A crab that can change its shape. They're said to be the offspring of the crab that pinched Hercules as he battled the Hydra.
- **Lightning Bird**- A familiar from South Africa with an affinity for lightning. Its beak can jump-start a car.
- **Mercat**- A shapeshifting feline with fur for land and scales in the water. They can live in lakes, rivers, or in the sea as well as on land. They must never completely dry out, or they will die.
- **Moon Hare**- A magical rabbit that gets power from its particular moon phase. They commonly bond with umbral magi.
- **Pharaoh's Rat**- These natural predators of dragon shifters are the size of ferrets and resemble a mongoose with more

fur. They have an affinity for space magic and can use it on occasion.

- **Pigeon**- Not as mundane as most think, some pigeons have an uncanny sense of direction due to their affinity for air magic.
- **Pricus**- An aquatic goat said to be descended from Capricorn. They can warp time even better than Gnomes.
- **Pure Faeries**- Creatures who spring to life from magical sources in the Under. They are genderless, and their type and ability depend on place of origin. They're associated with only one court, although they will work together to defeat a common enemy.
- **Sand Cat**- A feline that lives in the desert, able to go for weeks without water. Earth magic lets them do this.
- **Sha**- A magical desert dog from Egypt. Sha are the size of mundane toy breeds with short hair and small pointy ears. They could pass for mundane except for their blue tongues. They are attracted to anything undead.
- **Sphinx**- A magic cat with an affinity for fire. The reason they're hairless is that they're resistant to flames.
- **Strix**- A venomous owl with an affinity for poison. Female striges have rounded tufts on their heads, while males have pointed ones.
- **Sumxu**- A lop-eared cat found only in northern China. They are masters of camouflage and have an affinity for several kinds of magic.

Places

- **The Academy**—Something between a community college and a military academy for extrahumans, the Academy is geared toward helping extrahumans who don't play well with mortals get ready to join a blended society. It's got divisions for learners of all ages, though they are housed separately.

- **Cherry Blossom School**- A dojo geared toward teaching extrahumans self-restraint, meditation, and how to temper their enhanced physical abilities with more mundane skills. It's been around for close to a hundred years, run by the Ichiro family. Mundane classes used to be offered as a front but now are a separate division.
- **Ellicot City Magitechnic**- A prep school for magi and psychics specializing in magipsychic technology. It's located outside Baltimore.
- **Gallows Hill School**- Traditionally for shifters, this prep school in Salem recently opened its doors to changelings and other extrahumans not categorized as magi or psychics.
- **Hawthorn Academy**- A preparatory school for magi in Salem. Its campus is in the space between the mortal realm and the Under, giving it unrivaled privacy. They specialize in teaching familiar magic.
- **Providence Paranormal College**- A school founded just one year after Brown University and located right in its shadow. Providence Paranormal used to admit only magi and psychics, but it's been accepting all types of extrahumans ever since Henrietta Thurston became headmistress. There has been trouble since then for students and faculty, leading people to believe dissenters are sabotaging the school.
- **Trout Academy**- A prestigious preparatory school for changelings with magic, recently open to magi and magical shifters. Its campus is located in South County and has been operating in some form or another since Rhode Island Colony was founded.
- **The Under**- The faerie realm. It's been divided into two parts ever since the Sidhe Queen and the Goblin king split up thousands of years ago. Mortals don't age in the Under, but it's a dangerous place for them to be. Getting lost means never being seen again, and it's easy to get indebted to

something nasty while trying to get through or out of the Under.

- **Wolf Messing Prep**- An institute for psychics to learn to control their skills before heading to college.

Events

- **The Big Reveal**- The term used for the 1990s, when the world discovered magic was real and extrahumans existed. The decade was marked with fear as everyone adjusted to the changes. Since the 21st Century, law and technology work for both humans and extrahumans.
- **Boston Internment**- A reaction by Boston government officials to the disappearance and suspected trafficking in extrahumans, especially shifters. All registered extrahumans in Boston lived on barges for close to a month under guard by the Boston Police. The traffickers got their hands on some magical gadgets, rendering the protection useless. Few survived.

THANK YOU!

Thank you for reading! If you loved this book, please leave a review. You can find my other work by clicking the links below, going to **my website** or visiting my **Author Central page**.

ALSO BY D.R. PERRY

Providence Paranormal College

Bearly Awake (Book 1)

Fangs for the Memories (Book 2)

Of Wolf and Peace (Book 3)

Dragon My Heart Around (Book 4)

Djinn and Bear It (Book 5)

Roundtable Redcap (Book 6)

Better Off Undead (Book 7)

Ghost of a Chance (Book 8)

Nine Lives (Book 9)

Fan or Fan Knot (Book 10)

Hawthorn Academy

Familiar Strangers (Book 1)

Gallows Hill Academy

Year One: Sorrow and Joy (coming soon)

For other books by DR Perry please see her Amazon author page.

CONNECT WITH THE AUTHOR

Website: https://www.drperryauthor.com/

Join her newsletter!

Find more of D.R. Perry's books on Amazon.

OTHER LMBPN PUBLISHING BOOKS

To be notified of new releases and special promotions from LMBPN publishing, please join our email list:

http://lmbpn.com/email/

For a complete list of books published by LMBPN please visit the following pages:

https://lmbpn.com/books-by-lmbpn-publishing/

9 781649 718341